AYLMER VANCE:
GHOST-SEER

AYLMER VANCE
GHOST-SEER

Alice and Claude Askew

WORDSWORTH EDITIONS

In loving memory of
MICHAEL TRAYLER
the founder of Wordsworth Editions

1

Readers who are interested in other titles from
Wordsworth Editions are invited to visit our website at
www.wordsworth-editions.com

For our latest list and a full mail-order service contact
Bibliophile Books, 5 Thomas Road, London E14 7BN
Tel: +44 0207 515 9222 Fax: +44 0207 538 4115
e-mail: orders@bibliophilebooks.com

This edition published 2006 by
Wordsworth Editions Limited
8B East Street, Ware, Hertfordshire SG12 9HJ

ISBN 1 84022 539 4

Typeset in Great Britain by Antony Gray
Printed by Clays Ltd, St Ives plc

CONTENTS

The Invader

'What a wonderful moonlight night!' The words broke slowly from Aylmer Vance's lips, then he turned and looked at me strangely.

We were fellow-guests at the same little inn in Surrey, and we had just made our way out of the hot, stuffy parlour into a cool and perfumed garden.

'Does the moonlight ever affect you?' Vance asked. 'Does a night like this fill you with vague longings? Do you yearn to discover the secret of the universe – to know more than is good for man to know – perhaps to peer into the future?'

I nodded.

'Yes,' I answered slowly, then I turned to my companion. 'You have made a pretty deep study of spiritual phenomena, haven't you, Vance? I wish you would tell me something about the various experiences that have befallen you during the years you have been investigating on behalf of the "Ghost Circle".'

Vance shook his head. 'No, no,' he answered hurriedly. 'You wouldn't really be interested, Dexter. You are a level-headed barrister, my friend. You don't believe in spooks.'

'You're wrong there,' I retorted. The subject interests me profoundly, and tonight is just the night for a ghost story. There's a white, witching moon in the heavens – the pine trees look weird in the distance – and hark how the wind is sighing amongst their branches!'

Aylmer Vance smiled. He was a curious-looking man, tall and lean in build, with a pale but distinctly interesting face. His eyes were a bright blue, very sharp and keen, and he had long thin hands. There was a certain hardness about him – a chill austerity – but his voice, in strange contrast to his manner, was rich and flexible, and I had already fallen under the spell of his arresting personality.

We had first met at a dinner party in London about two months ago – a men's dinner – and I had been very interested in Aylmer Vance at the time. He had been pointed out to me as a ghost-seer. I had been told that ghost-hunting was his cult. And now, as luck would have it, we had tumbled across each other again, for we were both staying at the same little inn in Surrey. I had come down that day for some pike fishing, but I could not make out what had induced Aylmer Vance to spend a week at the Magpie Inn. But there he was, anyway.

We had recognised each other, dined by mutual consent at the same little round table, and now as we stood in the garden smoking our cigarettes I hoped that our acquaintance would end by developing into a friendship – a real friendship. But I had been told that Vance rarely made friends – that he lived a very solitary and self-contained life. He was quite well-off, and owned an old Georgian house situated somewhere in Essex, but he was not often in England. He was a great traveller – a born wanderer – and, needless to say, a bachelor.

'If you're really interested I don't mind telling you about three or four strange experiences that have befallen me during the years I have devoted to the investigation of spiritual phenomena.'

Aylmer Vance threw away his cigarette as he spoke. A queer look came over his face.

'I have certainly had some amazing adventures,' he continued. 'I have come across all sorts and conditions of men. I have been the means of detecting several instances of fraud and imposition on the part of so-called "mediums" – also of proving that natural causes are often responsible for the "haunting" that is supposed to go on in various houses. But I must admit that I have been absolutely baffled once or twice – unable to account for what I have seen with my own eyes, heard with my own ears.'

Vance paused and put a long thin hand upon my arm.

'Let us go and sit in the summer-house at the end of the garden, and I will tell you what happened about six years ago to two dear friends of mine – Annie Sinclair and her husband – for never have I been more impressed than by the Sinclair tragedy. In fact, it was the Sinclair affair that first induced me to take an interest in psychical research. The whole episode was so wrapped in mystery that even now I cannot explain it to myself. I am still in the dark as to what actually occurred.'

A curious, very intent note stole in Aylmer Vance's voice as he said the last words. A faraway look came into his eyes.

'Yes, I will tell you what happened to the Sinclairs,' he repeated. 'My story will certainly prove to you, if it proves nothing else, how dangerous it is to meddle with forces of which we know little.'

Still keeping his hand on my shoulder, he led me in the direction of the summer-house, which stood just at the bottom of the garden, and I remember how pungent the scent of the pines was – how overpoweringly pungent – and the wind made a queer rustling and sobbing amongst the branches of the pine trees – a low, monotonous moaning.

We settled ourselves down in the summer-house and I lit a cigarette. The moonlight was particularly brilliant that evening, I remember. It illuminated the whole garden. But the pine woods looked strangely blurred and black in the distance, and I felt rather eerie. Still I wished my companion would begin his story. I was sure it would be worth listening to.

'George Sinclair was my greatest friend when we were up at Oxford together,' Vance began, 'and after we left Magdalen we kept up our friendship, seeing each other constantly. Then I went abroad for two or three years. When I came back to England George had a great piece of news for me. He had just got engaged to be married to a Scotch girl. Her name was Annie Riddell.

'I went up to Scotland for the wedding. In fact, I was George's best man, and I'm bound to confess that I envied him his bride, for Annie looked a young goddess on her wedding day. She was tall and fair – rather a large woman, with a beautiful placid face and very sweet blue eyes; there was immense repose about her. George was just the opposite – very restless and excitable, dark, thin, and rather undersized; but they were crazily in love with each other, these two – as much in love as any man and woman could be, I think, and when I went to stay with them about six months later at George's place down in Wiltshire it was really delightful – in these days of matrimonial discontent – to see how fond a man and his wife could be of each other; not but what Annie gave away a little too much to George, I thought. She hardly appeared to have a will of her own – whatever he said was her law; but then George, for his part, was absolutely devoted to Annie. He thought her the most beautiful and perfect creature on God's earth – he worshipped her openly all day long, and Annie accepted her husband's homage with a bland serenity. If she hadn't been so beautiful I expect I should have thought her a dull woman, for she certainly lacked ideas, but she was so good to look at that one really hardly wanted to maintain a long conversation with her; you could stare at Annie for hours just as you could stare at a beautiful picture, and with the same pleasure.'

Vance paused for a minute. He seemed to be looking right into the pine wood, then he suddenly turned to me with one of his quick movements.

'Yes, they were intensely happy, those two, for the first three or four years of their married life – extraordinarily happy – but they began to be a bit disappointed by-and-by when no babies came – not that it made any difference to their love for each other. Their mutual sorrow knit them more closely together, if anything; but George, having no children to interest himself in, took it into his head to go in for occult research.

'The subject had always fascinated him, even from his boyhood, and then one day, as ill-luck would have it, George's attention was directed to the fact that he had a barrow on his property, by an archaeological friend of his who happened to be staying with the Sinclairs at Grey Towers. You know what I mean by a barrow, don't you? – one of those old British burial places of which there are still a few to be found in England.

'Well, George, egged on by his friend, started to dig up the barrow, and his efforts were rewarded, for he found two heavy gold armlets in it, and you cannot imagine how excited George got over this find. He had a theory that these armlets had belonged to some Druid priestess, and he took them to a medium, who spun him no end of a yarn about the woman who had once worn them; but she wasn't a priestess at all, the medium declared; she was a British princess, a very beautiful but jealous, black-hearted woman who had had a strange love affair and had been murdered by her lover.

'George drank in this yarn eagerly, and then what must the silly fool of a medium do but tell him that he possessed occult powers himself, and that Annie – who, needless to say, had always accompanied George on his visits to the medium – beautiful, quiet, meditative Annie, would make a very fine trance subject.

'Of course George, on hearing this, determined to exert his gifts, and Annie, who had always been like wax in his hands since the day of their marriage, went off obligingly enough into trances whenever he wanted her to. I don't think she was at all interested herself in occult subjects – at least not at the start, though she pretended to take an interest in them for George's sake, but she soon got frightened. She realised, being a sensible woman, that a certain amount of danger must always attend occult studies.

'Besides, she didn't like to feel – at least so she told me one day – that the spirits of dead men and dead women were talking through her to George, for Annie honestly believed that when she went off into one of her queer trances, she really became the vehicle of communication between the quick and the dead. She never doubted her own powers in that respect, but she was afraid of them.

'The whole thing began to prey on her after a time – to get upon her nerves, but George couldn't see this – or wouldn't see it. Evening after evening he insisted on putting Annie into a trance – he was never tired of experimenting with her. He didn't seem to realise that these experiments might have a disastrous effect upon his wife's health – that it might shatter Annie's entire system. He believed that in time the secrets of the other world would be revealed through her instrumentality – that a link would at last be established between the spirit world and our world.'

Vance paused. He threw away his cigarette – he drew a deep breath.

'Mark you, I don't blame George very much. He was an explorer into realms unknown, and, just like any other explorer, he was ready to sacrifice even his nearest and dearest, and I believe Annie's trances were quite genuine. I don't think for one instant she could have invented the things she said; besides, she wasn't that sort of woman – neither was she an hysterical subject.'

'So you think these trances were genuine?' I remarked.

'I do,' Vance replied. He bent forward and frowned and frowned; I thought how pale his face looked in the moonlight – how ghastly white. I noticed how tightly his hands were clenched; it was evident that the relating of this tale caused him deep emotion. 'I must own that I became profoundly interested myself in Annie's strange trances after a time, especially when the spirit of the British princess to whom the gold armlets found in the barrow had originally belonged began to take possession of Annie when she went off into her trances and talk through her mouth – and a mighty lot the princess had to say, too – queer, strange talk.

'She told us that she regretted most passionately that she was dead – that she longed to be alive again, walking the earth. She admitted that she was one of those restless, tormented spirits who, in psychical parlance, are known as "earth-bound spirits" – that all her desires were material, and she told George with brazen effrontery later on that she had fallen in love with him and that she would like to remain in possession of his wife's body – in fact, to take Annie's place in his life, and her language was plain and unvarnished, I can assure you – distinctly primitive. It gave me quite a shock to hear such words proceeding from Annie's lips, unconscious though she was, poor girl, of what the spirit who possessed her body for the time being was saying.'

Vance stirred in his seat – his lips twitched. He looked paler than I had thought it possible for a man to be.

'After the second or third séance, absorbing and interesting though they were, I got a bit uneasy in my mind. The whole thing struck me as horrible – repulsive, this dead woman invoking George in the most passionate language and having the audacity to suggest that she should try and keep Annie's gentle spirit out of its own tenement – continue to inhabit Annie's body. I said as much to George. I told him that I thought the séances had better stop, but he wouldn't listen to me; he was far too interested – far too keen on continuing his experiments.

'A fortnight later Annie spoke to him herself, however, and declined to go into any more trances. She declared that it had been a difficult matter to eject the princess's spirit after the last séance – that quite a fight had taken place between her own soul and the dead woman's soul, and that she was unwilling to run the risk of such a conflict again.

' "I assure you, George, I feel quite frightened," Annie exclaimed, "I am convinced that the princess wants to get possession of me. She'd like to live again in my body, and she's so strong – she's so frightfully strong – that it's difficult to drive her away after the trance is over – when I want to wake up – when you tell me to wake up."

'George laughed at this. He thought Annie was talking very foolishly, but he was seriously annoyed with her all the same for wanting to stop the séances – he insisted that they should continue – he was absolutely determined to proceed with his investigations.

'Well, Annie held out for a long time, but she gave way in the end. She was the sweetest woman on earth, I think, and though she made no secret of the fact that she simply loathed being put into a trance, George only laughed at her and finally got her to sit again, but Annie kept saying she would only sit once more. I don't know whether George believed that she would stick to her word, but anyway he asked me to go down to Grey Towers to be present at this last séance, but I couldn't go, so those two were just left to themselves and George's devil tricks.'

Vance rose abruptly to his feet. He looked very lean and haggard; the Sinclair tragedy seemed to have become his tragedy as well.

'Even now, after all these years, Dexter, I turn sick when I think of what happened down at Grey Towers. You see, I heard all about it afterwards – from George.'

Vance walked to the summer-house door. His thin face worked painfully. He kept clenching and unclenching his hands.

'They sat on a Saturday night – that is what George told me, for I had the whole story later on from his lips. He put Annie into a trance at once – Annie very nervous and unwilling – and after a bit the British woman came and took possession of her as usual. To make the connecting link as strong as he could, George had insisted that Annie should wear the gold bracelets dug up from the barrow, and so with these heavy links upon her arms, these relics from a barbarous past, Annie sat in her husband's study, a passive agent to what happened; but she repeated before the séance began what she had already said before. She told George that this would be the last time she would ever allow him to put her into a trance – that the coming back into her body was so difficult. She said just before she went off that she really would not sit again – that he mustn't ask her to, and that speech may have precipitated matters, of course, for I bet you the British woman knew that Annie meant what she said, and so she was aware that she would never again have the chance of speaking through Annie's lips – clothing her naked soul in Annie's body, and she determined to pit her strength against Annie's – to fight for what she wanted.'

'But what happened?' I interrupted eagerly. 'Did Mrs Sinclair find some difficulty in getting out of her trance? Did her heart fail suddenly – did she die that night?'

'I wish she had – I wish to God she had,' Vance answered bitterly. 'But worse – far worse – befell Annie. The British she-devil having taken complete possession of Annie's body absolutely refused to budge, for when George endeavoured to wake Annie up from her trance another woman – a passionate, primitive woman – stared at him out of his wife's eyes, and he knew that what Annie had feared had come to pass. A new tenant had taken up its habitation in her body – a tenant who refused to quit. There, Dexter, can you imagine a more grim and terrible situation; can you?'

Vance turned to me and put a hand upon my arm. I could feel how his fingers shook.

'I don't suppose you believe my story – it sounds pretty incredible – I don't think I believe it myself; but George swore to me that he knew Annie's gentle loving spirit couldn't get back into her body – that the British woman wouldn't turn out. Why, he declared that Annie's face changed before his eyes – that a devilish expression came into it, and to add to the sickening horror of the whole scene, the woman who called herself his wife began to make violent love to him – fierce, unrestrained love, and he had to suffer her hot, burning kisses; he couldn't tear himself away from her arms, and presently the woman demanded food and drink and ate ravenously, and then she began to croon and sing to herself, and George swore that he seemed to hear people singing outside the house, answering her – the low murmur of innumerable voices. It was just like a nightmare – an awful nightmare.

'It was hours that night before the woman fell asleep, and she gripped George's hand in her sleep – she held on to him as if she would never let him go, and when she woke up at dawn she began to sing to herself, some queer outlandish chant, and she sang as she brushed her hair, the wonderful pale gold hair that had always been one of Annie's greatest charms, and George, lying in bed, shivered, and lay there shivering and shaking, watching a beautiful woman combing her beautiful hair, but afraid of her – afraid.'

Vance hesitated, then he gave a queer hoarse laugh.

'I know what you're thinking. You are telling yourself that in all probability Annie Sinclair had got into a queer mental condition, thanks to all the séances that her husband had been insisting on, and that would account for her changed looks and manner – the singular way she was behaving – and no doubt George was feeling a bit queer and shaky himself – as nervous as a cat – frightened of his crazy wife, the wife who was apparently going off her head. That's the rational view to take of the situation isn't it – the most feasible view?'

'I don't altogether agree with you,' I retorted. 'We know that there have been several authenticated cases of demoniacal possessions.' I hesitated, then added, not looking at Vance as I addressed him, 'Did you see Mrs Sinclair after the – the séance?'

'Yes, I went straight down to Grey Towers on the receipt of an urgent telegram from George, and I felt when I met Annie as though I was meeting a stranger – and a strange woman who was always on her guard, but I dared not admit as much to George. I pretended that there was nothing amiss. Good Lord, man, what else could I do? But I was conscious all the time that some evil spirit had taken up its habitation in Annie's beautiful body – a wicked, baneful spirit – and the leer in Annie's eyes made me feel sick – I could hardly bear to look at her, and such a cruel smile played about her lips. She watched George just as a cat watches a mouse, and her hands were never still – those dreadful restless hands of hers. She walked with a stride, not as Annie used to walk, and her clothes seemed to hang on her awkwardly – Annie's clothes.'

Vance sat down again on the seat by my side. He was breathing
hard; I could see that little beads of perspiration had broken out on
his forehead, and he shivered, for all that it was such a hot evening.

'Wasn't it horrible, Dexter?' he whispered hoarsely. 'Wasn't it
horrible? You see, George and I were absolutely certain that Annie's
body had been possessed by a she-devil, and we knew that Annie's
soul – her sweet, gentle, loving soul – was trying its hardest to get
back to its earthly habitation, only the intruder wouldn't go, and we
both knew that she was trying to come back to us and that she just
couldn't; and we were aware – tragically aware – that as so often
happens in this world, evil was conquering goodness. But the awful
reflection, from George's point of view, was that he had deliberately
played into evil's hands – that he himself had brought this terrible
thing to pass – that it was his work – his.'

'Good Lord – how ghastly for the poor chap!' I muttered the
words low, half under my breath. Listening to Vance it was impossible to disbelieve the story he was telling me – he spoke with
such extraordinary conviction; then I leaned forward eagerly. 'Go
on, Vance – what was the end of it all?'

'The end.' Vance drew a deep breath. 'Well, it wasn't a pretty end,
Dexter.' He rose to his feet again; he looked absolutely livid in the
moonlight. 'I stayed at Grey Towers for about a week – I simply
couldn't have borne to remain there another day, for that creature –
that thing who inhabited Annie's body – was beginning to show
herself in her true colours. It was a barbaric woman whom George
had for a wife now – a woman who loved cruelty for cruelty's sake.
Why, she half killed George's dog one day because the poor brute
wouldn't come to her when she called it – and can you wonder? She
beat the dog with a stick till George got hold of her by the wrists and
dragged her off to her own room, and I don't know what passed
between them there – I don't even like to think of it, but I honestly
believe that George beat her – beat her as she had beaten the dog, for
when she came down she looked cowed. But she killed a bird the next
day – Annie's pet canary – walked up to the cage, took the bird out
and wrung its neck deliberately, and all because its singing annoyed
her. Can you wonder that I came away from Grey Towers that
afternoon? – And yet perhaps I ought to have stayed for George's
sake – for Annie's.'

Vance folded his arms. He drew another deep, half-sobbing breath.

'I heard from George a fortnight later. He told me that things
were going from bad to worse – that the woman – for that was how

he referred to her – had ridden Annie's favourite mare pretty well to death – that the servants had all given notice at Grey Towers, explaining that they couldn't understand the strange change that had come over their mistress – her ugly ways.

'Then George went on to say in his letter that he intended to put the woman into a trance that night and try and eject the evil spirit out of Annie's body, but I knew, even as I read George's letter – something seemed to tell me – that the woman would never consent to be put into a trance. She would be too clever for that – too cunning. And I was right, for two days later I got another letter from George – a letter in which he explained that the woman refused to sit.

'She was becoming wilder and more barbaric than ever, he added. A curious atmosphere seemed to hang over Grey Towers – an atmosphere of evil – and he could hear strange sounds at night. The whole house seemed to be full of mutterings and rumblings. There had been a terrible thunderstorm the day before, and the storm seemed to have broken directly over Grey Towers, and the woman had stood by the window laughing at the storm. He had been obliged to send his two dogs away, they kept up such an incessant howling; and he was left with hardly a servant in the house. The neighbours seemed to realise that something strange was happening and stopped calling. He felt forsaken by God and man.'

Vance paused.

'I ought to have gone straight back to Grey Towers on receipt of that letter, Dexter – hurried to my poor friend at once – but I didn't – I just didn't. I wrote to George, however, a long letter, and I suggested that it mightn't be a bad thing if he called in a certain famous psychic investigator to his aid, who might be able to exorcise the evil spirit that had taken up its habitation in Annie's body. But George wouldn't do this. Perhaps he was shy of making his story public. Perhaps he hoped to conquer by himself.

'What he did was to remove himself and the woman from Grey Towers. He rented a little cottage at Dartmoor and he and the woman went down there by themselves, and then I suppose the fight began – the long fight between George and the woman – for you may be certain that day after day – night after night – he tried his level best to throw her into a trance. But the woman refused to let herself go – to be conquered – and you can imagine, can you not, Annie's spirit hovering vaguely in the background – a silent witness of what was going on – an anguished witness.

'They could keep no servants at the cottage. A village woman came in in the morning and did the cleaning and what simple cooking was required. And so the days passed – the long sultry midsummer days – and George ceased to write to me. He left me in the dark as to what was going on.'

Vance sank down on his seat again. He covered his face with his hands – those long, thin nervous hands of his.

'I couldn't stand George's silence, not knowing what was happening, and at last I determined to go down to Dartmoor. I wrote to George announcing I was coming, and asked if he could either put me up at the cottage or take a room for me in the village. But George wired back to me and told me not to come.

YOU CAN DO NO GOOD. (so the telegram ran) NO-ONE CAN DO US ANY GOOD. LEAVE US ALONE, PLEASE.

'So I left them alone. I – I left them alone.'

A long silence fell, a silence I dared not break. I could hear the wind shaking and rustling the branches of the pine trees, keeping up a dull moaning. I could smell the sharp pungent scent of the pines.

The moon suddenly went in behind a cloud, and Aylmer Vance and I were alone in the darkness, and I was glad that the moon had hid her face. I did not want to look at Vance at that moment, and I felt sure that he did not want to look at me.

'You wish to hear the end of the story, Dexter?'

'Yes, I do.'

'Well, two days after I got that telegram from George I was sitting in the smoking-room of my club, when I suddenly heard some newsboys running down the street, and they were shouting out at the top of their shrill cockney voices: " 'Orrible murder at Dartmoor – 'orrible murder at Dartmoor", and I knew at once what had happened.

'I went out and bought a paper and I read that a gentleman – a Mr George Sinclair, who had recently rented a small cottage on Dartmoor – had murdered his wife the night before – had stuck a knife into her heart as they sat alone in their little cottage parlour, and had blown out his brains a few hours later – shot himself just when the dawn was breaking.

'The romantic part of the murder from the journalistic point of view consisted in the fact that the murderer, after killing his victim, had carried the dead woman's body up to their bedroom, dressed the corpse in a rich white satin gown, combed out her long fair hair, lit any amount of candles, and arranged them round the bed, and had then gone out into the little garden and picked nearly every flower, strewing these flowers over the dead woman, piling them in great scented masses at her feet; and there was no motive for the crime – so the newspapers informed their readers. Oh, they made capital enough, did those newspaper johnnies, out of the Sinclair mystery, I can assure you. They fairly revelled in it for days. And they didn't know – not a clever chap amongst them – that I could have told them the true history of the crime if I had chosen to unlock my lips. But I didn't.

'I went straight down to Dartmoor, however, and I said goodbye to George and I said goodbye to Annie. Lovely and pleasant they had been in their lives till that devil woman came between them, and in their deaths they were not divided.

'They were buried on the same day. The jury, of course, brought in a verdict of "temporary insanity" in George's case. I wish they could have slept in the same grave, but popular sentiment forbade that. The murderer and his victim couldn't lie together; for the public didn't know that it was not his wife whom George Sinclair had stabbed through the breast on a warm midsummer night – that it was a strange woman, a woman who belonged to the Stone Age.'

Vance paused, then gave another of his odd, mirthless laughs. He let his hands drip from his face.

'Queer yarn, mine, isn't it, Dexter – a bit hard to swallow? I don't ask you to believe it – to credit it. George Sinclair and myself may both have been the victims of a terrible delusion. The constant sitting at séances may have effected a deterioration in Annie's character, which we wrongly attributed to demoniacal possession, or of course overwrought nerves would account for the hysterical rages into which she threw herself at times. It is quite on the cards that the Sinclair affair was no case of demoniacal possession. But it was a tragedy for all that, wasn't it – a ghastly tragedy?'

'The most ghastly tragedy,' I repeated. The moon came out at that moment, and as I looked at Aylmer Vance our eyes met. I bent forward and laid an impulsive hand upon his arm. 'You do believe, don't you?' I whispered hoarsely. 'You do believe that the dead woman's spirit – the spirit of the British woman – had got hold of Annie Sinclair's body? You feel as I feel – that George did right when he killed the woman whom the world believed to be Annie Sinclair?'

'I don't know – I can't say,' Vance answered. 'But I am certain of one thing – that George Sinclair and his wife would be alive today if George had not persuaded Annie to go in for those ghastly sittings – if he had left that barrow undisturbed – for it does not do to meddle with the burial places of the primitive dead. It's an unwise proceeding to have anything to do with an earth-bound soul – a soul whose desires are all of the earth, earthy. And Annie knew this, mark you, and felt it. She was wiser in her generation than George, but just because she was sweet and gentle – '

He paused, and did not finish his sentence. But he drew his hand hurriedly across his eyes, and I realised – the knowledge suddenly came to me – that in his own quiet, reserved way Aylmer Vance had loved his friend's wife, the woman who belonged heart and soul to her husband.

We walked out of the summer-house. The pine woods looked as dark and mysterious as ever. I was conscious that Nature guarded innumerable secrets from man – secrets which she was loth to give up.

My grasp tightened on Vance's arm.

'Vance,' I whispered, 'have you ever seen a ghost with your own eyes – a visitant from the other world?'

'Have I?' Vance smiled – a curious smile. 'I will tell you about a little ghost whom I once had the pleasure of meeting, tomorrow night if you feel inclined to stay on at the inn and have another day's pike fishing. Yes, I will tell you where I met Lady Green-Sleeves. And there's nothing tragic about this story, Dexter. It was merely a singular experience – a romantic episode.'

The Stranger

I reminded Aylmer Vance of his promise to tell me about the little ghost whom he called Lady Green-Sleeves next evening, for, needless to state, I had stayed on at the Magpie Inn for another day's pike fishing; in fact, I had determined to spend a week in Surrey, for I had found out from Vance that he would not be taking his departure before the end of the week, and I wanted to remain as long as he did – to see as much of my new friend as possible.

I had been thinking of the strange story Aylmer Vance had told me the previous evening – the tale of the Sinclair tragedy. The horror of it had got hold of me – haunted me all day long – and now, as we sat in the little parlour of the quaint, old-fashioned inn, I wondered what other weird experiences Vance had gone through.

It was a wet night; no moon lit up the skies this evening, and heavy rain was falling – drenching rain. The weather had suddenly turned much colder – so damp and chilly that our worthy landlady had lit a fire, and I confess that the sight of that crackling fire pleased me. Besides, the parlour smelt rather musty; a fire in the room would do all the good in the world.

Vance drew up a big armchair to the hearth when we entered the parlour after dinner. He held out his hands to the cheerful blaze, a slow smile playing about his thin lips.

'I call this very comfortable,' he exclaimed. 'Very comfortable indeed. We will send for a bottle of port presently. We will drink old wine and we will crack old jokes. We will forget that it is raining and that the wind is howling outside.'

'And you will tell me all about Lady Green-Sleeves?' I interrupted. 'We will drink a toast to her – a toast to her sweet memory – for I am sure that she was gentle and young and fair.'

'Lady Green-Sleeves was small and dark, a little, eager, twinkling flame; but I am not going to tell you about her tonight. We will leave that for another evening – a warm, star-lit evening. I think I will tell you Daphne Darrell's story – Daphne Darrell's.'

He moved his chair closer to mine – he gazed right into the heart of the glowing fire. His very voice had changed – it was charged with a regretful tenderness.

'Yes, I will tell you Daphne Darrell's story tonight, and if it is a fine evening tomorrow, you shall hear all about little Lady Green-Sleeves – the dainty ghost I met face to face. I don't mind telling you my tales, Dexter, for you've a spark of romance in your heart. You're a dreamer as well as a shrewd barrister; but I wonder what you will make of Daphne Darrell's story? Anyway, the poetry of it will appeal to you – it must.'

He bent forward. The firelight flickered over his pale, thin face; he laughed softly to himself.

'The great elemental forces, Dexter – why do we no longer believe in them – the old gods and goddesses – the lost faiths? Either we are much wiser than our forefathers, or our forefathers were much wiser than us. But that's a question for the gods to decide – they who know.'

Vance paused – one of those long pauses to which I was getting accustomed – then he suddenly started and looked up at me.

'I was going to tell you about Daphne Darrell. I happened to be her guardian. She was the posthumous child of a cousin of mine, a young fellow who met his death under very tragic circumstances about six months after his marriage. He and his wife were pioneers of the open-air movement. They were immensely rich folk, but they liked to jog about the country in a big caravan during the summer, and live a sort of gipsy life.

'It was whilst they were on one of these caravan expeditions that the great tragedy happened. Robert Darrell, bathing in the Thames one morning, was suddenly seized with cramp and drowned before his wife's eyes. Poor Lucy Darrell was prostrate with grief at first, for she was absolutely devoted to her husband, but she kept up as bravely as she could for the sake of her unborn child. Nothing would induce her to go back to Darrell Court, however – my cousins had a fine place in Hampshire, I must tell you. She continued her nomad life all that summer, and the baby was actually born in the caravan, the caravan pitched for the night in Savernake Forest.

'Poor Lucy died within a few days of her child's birth, and perhaps it was just as well, for she was a heartbroken woman; but it seemed a little rough on Daphne – for the child, I must explain, was christened Daphne at her mother's request – to have lost both her parents in her infancy. However, an old aunt came forward – one of those dear, sweet, maiden ladies who are always ready to step into the breach in moments of difficulty, and Miss Jane Darrell volunteered to look after her little niece and make her home at Darrell Court. It was a bit of a sacrifice, I can tell you, for the old lady had a charming house in London and a big circle of friends.

'She was a delightful old gentlewoman was Miss Jane, and it was a great pleasure to me to run down to Darrell Court whenever I found myself in England. It interested me greatly to watch my little ward in the various stages of her evolution. She was a very interesting child, strikingly original in her thoughts and ways, but she was the terror of her nurse and governess, for Daphne would never take the least trouble to learn her lessons, and it made her ill to be kept indoors. She would have liked to spend all her time in the woods and the stately park that fenced Darrell Court from the world. She hated indoor life, and Miss Jane gave way to Daphne in everything. She spoilt her niece shamefully; the consequence was that Daphne grew up lovely, but quite uneducated – a wild, woodland creature.'

'Was she very lovely?' I leaned back in my chair as I spoke. It was pleasant to sit in this warm, cosy little parlour and listen to the rain pelting outside, and the melancholy howling of the wind – interesting to watch Aylmer Vance as he talked, very interesting.

'Lovely – was Daphne Darrell lovely?' Vance laughed. 'Why, at eighteen she was the most beautiful creature that ever trod the earth! She was tall and slim as a young pine tree, with the most wonderful dark blue eyes and any amount of fair hair. Her face was pure Greek; she had a forehead – a brow – that Clytie herself might have envied. She was flawless – perfect; she reminded one of a nymph, so there was some reason for the pride Miss Jane took in her niece. There was no-one like Daphne in her eyes, and I can assure you that Miss Jane's opinion was shared by a good many people; for what did it matter if Daphne had never learnt her dates, if her spelling was atrocious, her knowledge of history nil, her French accent hopeless? She made other women in a room look dim when she walked in; she was the living incarnation of youth and strength. She had a clear, beautiful voice, that was not unlike the sound of rippling waters, and her laugh – why, woodland nymphs must have laughed like that when the world was young; our girls have lost the trick of it nowadays.

'She was very fond of me; a curious rapport prevailed between us – a strange comradeship; in fact, years ago – when Daphne was a child of eight or nine – she confided a great secret to me – a secret she had shrunk from telling anyone else, even Miss Jane. She whispered it into my ear one afternoon as we walked up and down the long green terrace walk – the terrace that stretched out in front of Darrell Court. She explained that she was in the habit of meeting someone in the woods – a tall youth, as far as I could make out – and playing with him.

' "I hide behind the bushes, and he runs after me," Daphne explained; "but he never catches me – I never let him. He is so tall and graceful, and so strong."

' "You mustn't play with strangers, Daphne," I remarked; "with strange young men. Is this youth a village boy?"

'Daphne shook her head. To this day I can remember the curious smile that played about her lips – the wise smile.

' "A village boy – oh, no!" she answered. "And yet he is not a stranger; I have known him – "

'She paused, and did not finish the sentence. A strange look came into her deep blue eyes – a look that puzzled and vaguely alarmed me.

'She would never tell me any more about the youth, except once, when I had taken her up to London to see the Academy. I remember her standing entranced in front of a statue by one of our rising young artists – a statue of the god Apollo.

' "Do you like this statue, Daphne?" I queried.

'The child – for Daphne was little more than a child – turned to me with shining eyes and flaming cheeks.

' "Like it?" she cried. "Why of course I do; it's so like him." She paused and laughed – shy, rather conscious laughter. "I mean like the stranger I meet in the woods sometimes – the stranger I play hide-and-seek with."

' "You mustn't be so fanciful, Daphne," I remember saying. "Of course, this is only a game of make-believe; you don't really meet anyone in the woods."

' "No, I suppose not," Daphne admitted. She spoke with a singular reluctance, and we did not refer to the subject again; but three years later, on Daphne's seventeenth birthday, she bought a small marble copy of the famous Apollo Belvedere statue, and put it on a small table in her bedroom, and there was always a vase standing in front of the statue; and the curious thing was that Daphne never put flowers in this vase, but only grass – the freshest, greenest, and juiciest grass she could find.

'By the time Daphne was nineteen there was hardly a young man in Hampshire who was not in love with her, but her choice finally fell on Anthony Halbert. Anthony's father and mother, Sir George and

Lady Melton, were devoted to Daphne. She had known the family all her life, for the two estates joined; also Miss Jane was very much in favour of the marriage, for she was an old friend of Tony's mother.

'Besides, Miss Jane felt – at least, so she confided to me afterwards – that it would be a very good thing if Daphne had a husband to look after her, for she was getting just a little out of hand. She did unconventional things that worried Miss Jane – worried her exceedingly. She would go off to the woods for whole days at a time, quite oblivious of the social engagements which her aunt had made for her – the garden-parties and tennis-parties which would have appealed to most young girls – the local race meetings.

'Daphne also insisted, during the spring and summer months, on sleeping out of doors. She had a hammock slung between the boughs of two high cedars on the lawn, and nothing would content her but she must sleep in this hammock. Notwithstanding all Miss Jane's entreaties, she absolutely refused to wear corsets – not that that mattered in the very least – her firm young figure needed no artificial support. Also, she had a marked aversion to wearing hats – it was difficult to persuade her ever to put one on; and she loved to take off her shoes and stockings and wade through long wet grass. She would throw herself down with a cry of the purest physical enjoyment amongst bracken; she loved to lie for hours on the lawn in the sunshine, hardly moving a finger – just sleeking her body in the hot sun-rays.

'Of course, these traits in Daphne's character were partly hereditary, but, all the same, Miss Jane was uncommonly glad when young Tony Halbert got Daphne's promise to marry him. She felt as if a great load had been taken off her shoulders – as if she had been relieved from an immense responsibility, for to look after Daphne the child was quite a different matter to looking after Daphne the woman; and the poor old lady realised this – realised it keenly.'

Vance paused and drew a deep breath, then he stroked his chin meditatively with his left hand. His eyes looked very dreamy and reflectful.

'Daphne wrote to me herself to announce her engagement. I had just returned to England from Egypt; I had been spending a fine time in Egypt, exploring some old temples, and I remember being profoundly struck by Daphne's letter, and dismayed.

I am engaged to be married to Tony Halbert, dear guardian – so the note began, as well as I can remember – and I am sure you will approve of my choice. Tony is absolutely devoted to me, and so are his people, and I am very, very fond of him; also, I think in many ways it would be a good thing for me to marry and settle down, as Aunt Jane puts it.

Come and stay with us as soon as you can, guardy dear; and please give me away at my wedding. We are going to be married quite soon – in about six weeks' time.

DAPHNE

P.S. You are a dreadfully clever man, guardy, and you investigate, don't you, for the Ghost Circle? So will you please tell me what people ought to do when they see visions – visions in broad daylight? Ought they to regard themselves as mentally afflicted, or believe that their eyes, for some purpose, have been opened? Do you think this world only belongs to the living, or do you believe that the past still has some hold on it – some claim? And have we lived before, or are we just ourselves?

'I answered Daphne's letter in person. I do not mind confessing to you, Dexter, that it worried me – that I felt distinctly uneasy, but when I arrived at Darrell Court I was quite reassured.

'Daphne was playing tennis with her fiancé, and she looked splendidly healthy, exceedingly happy, not at all the sort of girl to indulge in delusions. She threw down her racquet directly she caught sight of me, and ran across the lawn to meet me, Tony following her. She seemed in wonderful spirits, and she could talk of nothing else but her forthcoming wedding. She told me, all in a breath, where she and Tony were going for their honeymoon – what beautiful presents friends were sending them – how there was to be a presentation from the tenantry in a day or two's time, and Daphne was especially eloquent about the dance that was to be given at Darrell Court the night before the wedding.

'"I am having the dance the night before," she exclaimed, "because I think it's such a silly thing to have the dance after the wedding, when the bride and bridegroom have gone. Besides, Tony and I both love dancing. There's to be a big ballroom built out on the lawn, and we are having the Blue Hungarian Band, and it's sure to be a lovely midsummer night. I hope you will enjoy the dance, guardy – I think we must open it together."

'I laughed and shook my head.

'"No, Daphne," I answered. "I think it will be Tony's place to lead you out. Now, if that young man of yours can spare you to me for a few minutes, I think we will take a turn together, for your old guardian has all sorts of questions to ask you."

'Tony surrendered Daphne to me at once. He was a tall, good-looking young fellow, with an honest face and a pair of good, brown eyes. He was close on six feet in height, a very muscular young Englishman – a sweetheart to be proud of.

'I led Daphne into the rose garden. It was a quaint, old-fashioned little garden, sheltered by high yew hedges, and roses bloomed there in great masses – the air was heavy with their fragrance. There was a marble seat in one corner of the rose garden, and Daphne and I sat down. She was all in white, I remember, and, as usual, she wore no hat; her hair shone in the sunlight gold. Her beautiful throat was bare, and she wore no rings on her hands; she had refused – so I learnt afterwards – to wear an engagement ring.

' "You are quite happy, Daphne, are you not?" I began. "I don't think you could possibly be engaged to a nicer young fellow. I have always liked Tony Halbert, and I have never heard anything but good of him; in fact, your guardian highly approves of the match you are making – he considers it a most suitable one."

'Daphne looked at me queerly.

' "That's how I feel myself, guardy – that I am doing a very sensible thing in marrying Tony, for I could never marry anyone who was nicer – in fact, half so nice; but – " She paused. Colour suddenly flooded her face, warm colour. She turned to me nervously, a little shyly. "Did you think me mad when I wrote that postscript to my letter, guardy – quite mad?"

'I shook my head.

' "No, Daphne," I answered, "but I felt a little puzzled by that postscript. What does it mean, my dear, tell me frankly, what does it mean?

' "I don't know myself." She shook her head. "Except that I fancy I must suffer from hallucinations at times – ridiculous hallucinations. Do you remember when I was quite a little girl, guardy, how I told you one day about the beautiful stranger whom I said I used to meet in the woods and play hide and seek with behind the trees and bushes? Well, I expect you thought I was romancing, telling stories, but I wasn't. I really used to meet that stranger, and – and I meet him still."

' "My dear Daphne!" I looked at my ward sternly. "You really mustn't say such things to me – such absurd things."

' "But it's the truth, guardy. I do meet someone in the woods. I have never spoken to him, nor has he spoken to me; I have never even touched his hand, and I always call him the stranger to myself, except when I call him the – the god."

'She lowered her voice to a faint whisper. An extraordinary look had come into her eyes – a look that frightened me.

' "He's glorious – so glorious that I cannot believe him to be mortal man. He frightens me a little now, though he never frightened me when I was a child. He is as bright as a flame is bright, his shining flesh gleams like marble through the green bushes. His eyes draw me – compel me, and yet they are fierce eyes – very fierce."

'She checked herself abruptly.

' "Tell me that it is all nonsense, guardy – that it is only an hallucination of mine. That I shall forget all about my stranger – my god – once Tony has got me in his own safe keeping."

' "Of course it is all nonsense, Daphne," I replied. "You fancied that you met this – this stranger when you were a child, and you have kept up the fancy all your life, and it's become a sort of delusion with you – an unhealthy delusion. But, as you truly say, once you are married to Tony you will put all this nonsense out of your head; you will have to."

' "Yes, I shall have to." She gave a quiet little nod, then she crept closer to me on the seat. "Guardy, I must tell you something else. I had better confess straight out that though I am awfully fond of Tony I am not the least bit in love with him. It's the stranger I love; why, I should die with sheer delight if he kissed me, I think, but he is only a dream, I suppose, a dream."

'I took Daphne by one of her cold hands. I looked straight into her eyes.

' "Child, madness lies in such dreams," I cried. "Do you realise that? – Madness. You must forget all about this stranger – you must put him out of your life, out of your thoughts; but with Tony to help you, my dear, you will soon succeed in conquering this hallucination. Thank God you are going to be married, Daphne, and that the wedding is fixed to take place soon." '

Aylmer Vance rose from his chair, and began to walk up and down the room. His long arms hung down by his side, his face looked thinner and paler than ever.

'Just listen to the rain, how it beats against the windows. Does my story interest you, Dexter?'

'Distinctly. Please go on – don't stop at such an exciting moment. What did Miss Darrell say in answer to your speech?'

'Very little, nor did she appear at all disposed to continue the conversation. She merely gave me a faint, shadowy smile; and Tony turned up a few minutes later and carried her back to the tennis court to finish the game I had interrupted. They ran off together, laughing like two children, but I thought Daphne looked very distrait during dinner. She hardly ate or drank anything, and she kept staring vaguely through the open window – gazing in the direction of the wise green woods. She wanted to go out for a walk after dinner, to roam with Tony in the grounds, but Miss Jane asked her to sing to us instead – I must hear how wonderfully Daphne's voice had improved, the old lady said. But Daphne wouldn't sing, and she grew more and more restless as the evening wore on. She even seemed in a hurry to get rid of Tony; certainly she did not press him to stay when he finally rose to depart, nor were their *adieux* very prolonged.

' "You are not going to sleep out of doors again this evening, are you, darling?" Miss Jane asked, rather anxiously, as she kissed Daphne good night a few minutes later. "I can hardly bear to think of you in the darkness – your hammock swinging from those big cedar trees."

' "Why, it's lovely out of doors, Aunt Jane," Daphne answered. "I couldn't sleep indoors – I really couldn't – on such a hot night as this, and I'm not a bit frightened. Why should I be frightened? Do you think someone will steal out of the woods and carry me away – some stranger?"

'She laughed and left the room laughing. Miss Jane and I looked at each other anxiously.

' "Isn't she a queer girl?" Miss Jane exclaimed. "Oh, I shall be thankful, Mr Vance, when Daphne is safely married to dear Tony."

' "And I shall be thankful too," I answered, and I meant what I said.'

Vance walked back to his chair again. The fire was beginning to burn down; he put some more coals on, and I noticed that his hands were shaking a little.

'Well, you want to hear the rest of my yarn, I supposed, Dexter? I left Darrell Court next morning. I had only been able to arrange to come down for the night – I had a lot of business to attend to, you see, having so recently returned to England. But I promised Daphne that I would come back the day before the wedding in order to be present at her dance, and I gave her a word of warning as we said goodbye.

' "Don't think any more of that dream of yours, Daphne – that silly delusion. Forget it, my dear – keep your thoughts fixed on Tony."

'Daphne smiled and nodded her head.

' "That's all right, guardy," she answered. "You can trust me to be quite sensible in the future."

'She waved her hand to me gaily enough as I drove away, and how was I to guess that even then her thoughts were turning to the stranger in the forest – that she was deceiving all of us, and perhaps herself?

'I returned to Darrell Court for the dance, as I had arranged to do. I found the house packed with young people; four of the bridesmaids were staying there and several of the groomsmen. The sound of wedding bells was in the air, a happy excitement prevailed, and Daphne herself seemed the gayest of the gay, not that I saw much of her; she seemed to be always surrounded by a bevy of girls – pretty girls, who chattered at the top of their voices.

'She sought me out of her own free will just before dinner, however. I had dressed early, and had gone down to the study, feeling a little out of things, for the young people were having it all their own way in the drawing-room; they were dancing there already.

' "Guardy, I want to speak to you." Daphne spoke in low, rather hesitating tones, then she shut the study door behind her and walked up to me. She looked more beautiful than I had ever seen her. She was dressed all in white, as became tomorrow's bride, and her gown clung tightly to her glorious young figure. She wore no jewels beyond a fillet of pearls in her hair; but the expression in her face troubled me – there was such a yearning look in her eyes – such a strange look.

' "What's the matter, Daphne?" I asked. "My dear, you are not un-happy, are you?"

' "I am very unhappy, guardy." She bowed her head; two big tears rolled down her cheeks. "I don't love Tony, I shall never love Tony, and I am going to marry him tomorrow; and he will take me away from all that I care for most – from my freedom, my solitude, my woods. I shall never be able to spend long days by myself in the future, alone with the wild things. I shall have to become domest-icated; I shall be a wife – perhaps later on a mother."

'She paused, then added, speaking very quickly and nervously:

' "I ought never to have become engaged, I see that now. I ought always to have belonged to myself. I oughtn't to have been afraid of my dreams, my fancies, and anxious to have them dispelled, for what can Tony give me in exchange – what can he give me?" She threw back her head – she gazed at me defiantly.

' "Tony can give you love," I answered steadily. "He can give you reality."

' "I want neither." She laughed, queer broken laughter. "I want, guardy, what I shall never find – what I never can find now."

'She swayed from foot to foot, such a slim young figure, then she suddenly sank on her knees and raised her white arms high above her head.

' "Oh, my dreams – my beautiful dreams," she moaned, "my lost dreams! Have I got to say goodbye to them forever tonight, and goodbye to the stranger, goodbye to the lover who has never kissed me, who never will kiss me, but whose kisses I desire above all things, whose love I crave for?"

'She trembled violently. I remember putting my hand upon her shoulder and feeling how her flesh quivered. I also recollect that I shook Daphne – shook her fiercely.

' "Child, don't talk so madly," I cried. "You forget yourself; you don't know what you are saying. You are overtired, you are hysterical tonight – you must be hysterical."

'Daphne swayed slowly to her feet, then a film seemed to gather over her eyes. She laughed, soft, broken laughter.

' "Yes, that's what's the matter with me, guardy," she murmured. "I am hysterical – overwrought. I have been trying on clothes all this last week without ceasing, and there's been so much to see to with regard to the wedding. I must pull myself together now. I shall be all right for the dance tonight, and quite all right tomorrow; and of course I don't want to fail Tony at the last minute – I wouldn't do that for anything. Think how Tony loves me, and what a dear he is!"

'She ran out of the room before I could say another word, and joined her guests in the drawing-room, and I got no opportunity of talking to her during dinner.

'Directly after dinner the entire house-party made their way in gay procession to the huge marquee that had been built out on the lawn and turned into a temporary ballroom. The band struck up a waltz as we entered. Tony caught Daphne round her waist and spun her into the middle of the floor, and in a few minutes the whole house-party was dancing, and Daphne's laugh rang out gaily as Tony waltzed her round. It was hard to believe that I had seen her on her knees in the study only an hour before, indulging in passionate invocation.

'Guests began to arrive. Miss Jane insisted on introducing me to various ladies, with whom I was in duty bound to dance, but at last I managed to sneak off by myself to enjoy a quiet cigarette on the terrace. It was a stiflingly hot evening, and I had rather a bad headache. I fancied there was a storm about; once or twice I thought I heard the distant rumble of thunder, but I hoped the storm would not come on before morning. Still there were not so many stars out as there had been an hour ago.

'I lit my cigarette, and proceeded to stroll up and down the terrace. Suddenly I caught sight of Daphne's figure in the distance, stealing out of the ballroom, and she was alone, much to my amazement; she had evidently deserted her partner. She ran like a hare across the lawn – ran straight in the direction of the woods that slope to the right of Darrell Court; I determined to follow at a safe distance, and see for myself what would happen in those woods – and I did see.'

A curious change came over Aylmer Vance's voice as he said the last words. His whole body appeared to stiffen as he sat in his chair. A strange thrill ran through me; I sat up erect in my chair, too.

'Daphne gained the wood without noticing that I was following her. She ran at a breathless pace, as if she was in the greatest hurry, and when we entered that dark wood, Dexter, I was distinctly conscious of the sound of music – the music of the flute. I told myself at once – for I hope I am a sensible man – that of course it was merely the echo of the dance music that I was listening to, and I suppose that's what it was.'

Vance hesitated, and bit his lips.

'I hardly know how to describe to you what happened next. I don't want you to think me a lunatic, but it seemed to me as though the wood was full of people, and yet I could see no-one actually; but every now and then I caught glimpses of the white arms of girls. I could hear what sounded like soft girlish laughter, and once a long tress of hair seemed to be blown right across my face; I could have sworn to this at the time, but perhaps it was only my fancy. Maybe it was merely some dark bough I brushed against – some soft, sweet-scented bough, for everything was so vague, Dexter, so hopelessly indefinite, and yet, if I can make you understand, so real.'

Vance half-closed his eyes. He was talking in very slow, measured tones; I strained my ears to catch every word.

'Daphne ran on right into the heart of the wood. It was getting very dark overhead. I was certain that the storm would break quite soon, the thunderstorm I had been anticipating. The angry rumbles of distant thunder had grown much louder lately, but the strange thing was I never once thought of calling to Daphne to come back with me to the house, or of warning her that a storm was approaching. Perhaps I was no more myself that night than she was – maybe we were both fey, but I was conscious as I followed her through the wood that there were strange powers abroad that evening – strange forces. I felt curiously excited – oddly stirred. A longing to say goodbye to civilisation and to conventionality came over me. I yearned for greater freedom than I had ever known – for a more intimate knowledge of nature. I felt it would be delightful to cast my clothes from me and bathe in the dew-moistened grass. I forgot that I was a staid and respectable man of forty; all the feelings of youth came back – the sublime intoxication of youth.'

Vance's head dropped forward on his breast. His eyes were completely closed.

'Well, Dexter, I must make an end of my story, or I shall weary you to death. Daphne suddenly fell down on her knees, just as she had done in the study, and she held up her white arms and seemed to cry to someone to come to her – a long, passionate, half-inarticulate cry, and it was the cry of a woman calling to her beloved, summoning him to her, and as I am a living man, Dexter, something – someone – came in answer to Daphne's cry. He – for it was a man – seemed to shoot down from the branches of a high fir tree, and he was white and shining and nude. A fierce brightness seemed to diffuse from him, and he carried a bow in his hand – he was the archer.'

Vance raised his head as he said the last words, opened his eyes, and stared me in the face.

'I am not asking you to believe me, Dexter – I know that my tale sounds too incredible – but I tell you when I saw this flash of light descending, as it were, upon Daphne, I covered my face with my hands, and fell to the ground myself, for what right had I, a mere man, to spy upon this meeting of a maid and an immortal? Yes, I crouched abashed to the ground, and as I did so a great thunderclap seemed to shake the earth to its foundations – such a thunderclap.'

Vance bent forward in his chair and put a hand upon my arm.

'There's very little more to tell you now,' he whispered. 'There was no wedding at Darrell Court the next day, for the tragic reason that the bride had been struck by lightning the night before. We don't believe, you and I, being wise, sensible, practical men, that it was a lover's kiss that killed her – a lover's burning kiss; and yet the lightning had hardly scarred her sweet body, though it had struck her dead.'

'What a horrible – what a ghastly tragedy!' I interrupted. A cold shiver ran through my spine as I spoke, but Aylmer Vance shook his head.

'You're making a mistake, my dear friend. There was nothing really tragic about Daphne Darrell's death. It was the fate she would have chosen, I have no doubt, if she had been given her choice, for remember – if we are to believe her own story – she was not the least in love with Tony Halbert; and think what a loveless marriage would have meant to a girl of Daphne's temperament! She met her dream and her death at the same time. Besides, have you forgotten, Dexter, that "those whom the gods love die young"?'

I made no answer, but as I watched Aylmer Vance kneel down in front of the fire to warm his hands, I ventured to ask him a question.

'Do you believe that the old gods are dead, Vance? – do you really believe that?'

Vance smiled – a strange inscrutable smile.

'They are dead to some,' he answered, 'but they are alive to others.'

Lady Green-Sleeves

'As you're not fishing – this being the Sabbath Day – would you like to walk as far as the pine woods with me, Dexter, and I'll tell you the story of Lady Green-Sleeves – that is, if you're not getting bored with my yarns?'

Aylmer Vance smiled, his quiet, wise smile, as he addressed me. He had just wandered into the quaint old-fashioned garden of the Magpie Inn, and had found me lounging in a basket chair – basking in the sunshine, for the rainy night had been followed by a glorious morning, and, needless to say, I sprang to my feet at once, for the two queer tales that Vance had already told me had made me very curious to hear about Lady Green-Sleeves, and I said as much to my friend.

'So you're quite ready to wander to the pine woods with me, and you'd like to be told about my little ghost – the daintiest ghost a man could ever have the pleasure of meeting. There's nothing dreadful or tragic in this tale – 'tis sheer romance; you'll enjoy it, Dexter – you'll enjoy it.'

Vance slipped his arm familiarly through mine, then he laughed softly.

'You're such a surprising person, Dexter. Who, to look at you, would imagine for one instant that you are a dreamer of dreams – a firm believer in spooks? You are such a typical barrister, as far as appearances go; yet here I am pouring out all my adventures to you – every uncanny adventure I have ever had – for you do believe in my stories. There's nothing of the sniffing sceptic about you; that's why I am able to talk so freely – to open out my heart.'

'I couldn't fail to believe your stories,' I answered slowly; 'no-one could who watched your face whilst you are relating them – heard your voice; and now I am impatient – most impatient – to hear all about Lady Green-Sleeves.'

'Wait till we reach the pine woods. I'll throw myself down on a bed of pine needles, close my eyes, and you shall have the whole story as it occurred. It may tax your credulity more than the other tales, though; it's so dreamy and so unexplainable.'

Vance lowered his voice. I could feel the nervous trembling of his thin, sensitive fingers as he clutched my arm, and I was more than ever conscious of the strange sympathy that existed between us. I knew – something seemed to tell me – that we were going to be friends, firm friends, for the rest of our lives, and I hoped that Vance would ask me to be his companion during some of his future expeditions to haunted houses.

It took us about ten minutes to walk to the woods. The spicy scent of the pines filled the air; hot sunshine poured down upon a world that was literally a riot of green this morning, and I felt – I could not help feeling – how good it was to be alive. I said as much to Vance, and he laughed; I confess I was extremely puzzled by his laughter at times, but I understood why he had laughed after he told me his story – I understood quite well.

Vance threw himself down on a great heap of pine needles, just as he had said he would – a soft, scented heap, and I made myself a similar couch. We both lay luxuriating in the brilliant sunshine for a minute or two, then Vance bent towards me. His face looked much softer than I had ever seen it, a vague smile played about his mouth.

'Now I will tell you all about my Lady Green-Sleeves. I met her about twelve years ago, and the evening we spent together stands out with startling distinctness in my memory – such a rose-scented evening.'

'The evening you spent together?' I raised myself on my elbow and stared hard at Vance, wondering if I had heard aright. 'Why, did Lady Green-Sleeves' ghost pay the world such a long visit as all that? I thought ghosts only appeared for a few seconds and then vanished?'

Vance nodded his head.

'So did I; but I was wrong, it appeared – quite wrong; and now, with your leave, my good friend, I will continue my narrative.'

Vance paused. He had thrown himself down on his back. He was gazing straight up into a dazzlingly blue sky, and I knew he saw far more than I could see – that he was conjuring up the ghost of a little dead and gone lady – recalling a romantic episode.

'Well, Dexter, I must commence my story by explaining to you that I had not the least idea that my Lady Green-Sleeves was a ghost till she had made me her pretty curtsy and departed. I took her for a masquerader first of all – a dainty rogue of a masquerader; for, you see, I met her at a fancy dress ball, a big dance given by some very rich people in Yorkshire – a dance to which I had been taken by friends.'

Vance closed his eyes. His voice sounded very rich and musical; the dreamy smile still played about his lips.

'How well I remember that night, Dexter. It was a cold December evening, and we had to drive over nine miles to Arden Hall, for that was the name of the house where the dance was taking place. I felt very cross at being taken to the ball; I was not particularly fond of dancing, and I hated – as so many men do – the bother of having to go to it in fancy dress. I wore a Georgian suit; the coat was of plum-coloured satin, I recollect, with a white brocade waistcoat sprigged with silver, and my hostess had been pleased to compliment me on my appearance – I was ten years younger than I am now.'

Aylmer Vance paused. Looking at him as he lay on the ground, it was not difficult to guess that with his long, well-knit limbs he would cut a fine figure in Georgian costume, and that a white peruke would prove very becoming. There was certainly an old-world dignity about him, a polished refinement.

'Continue your story!' I exclaimed. 'I want to hear when you first caught sight of Lady Green-Sleeves. Your plum-coloured coat was very beautiful, I expect; but let us get to the lady.'

'I caught sight of her the moment I entered the hall. There was a great balcony running round it, and she was bending over the oak balcony gazing down into the hall below, watching the guests arrive, so I imagined she must be one of the house-party. Our eyes met, and I can tell you, Dexter, a thrill ran through me; my heart suddenly began beating wildly. I made up my mind I'd contrive to get introduced to Lady Green-Sleeves that evening, for that was the name I gave her to myself – Lady Green-Sleeves.'

Vance raised himself suddenly to a sitting position. His eyes were wide open now, but he did not look at me; he gazed straight ahead, and I knew who he was gazing at, for his smile deepened; he had forgotten me for the moment – he had conjured up a memory.

'Was Lady Green-Sleeves very pretty?'

I put the question rather diffidently. I hated to arouse Vance from his reverie, yet I longed to hear the rest of the story.

'Pretty! That's a poor word to describe Lady Green-Sleeves. She was adorable; but I think it was her daintiness that most appealed to me – her delicious daintiness. She had a sweet face, a roguish smile; her eyes were as violet and velvety as purple pansies. Her brown curls, innocent of powder, clustered becomingly about a pure low forehead, peeping from under a lace hood, a hood fastened under Lady Green-Sleeves' soft little chin with a rosebud. She was very young – barely seventeen, I thought – a sweet child, who would blossom presently into a delightful woman; and I suddenly found myself wishing that I was a few years younger – more of an age with this brown-haired beauty.'

Vance played idly with a handful of fir cones; a longing look had come over his face; then he sighed heavily.

'I hardly know how to describe what Lady Green-Sleeves had on. Her dress struck me as being distinctly fantastic, but I suppose it belonged to the Georgian period, like my own. Her hooped petticoat was of fine creamy silk, and over this petticoat she wore a sort of looped-up green mantle, with long wide sleeves. As far as I can recollect, her bodice was of the same creamy stuff as her petticoat, fastened in front with a green lace. She wore a small bunch of pink roses at her breast, and her green mantle was looped up with a slightly bigger bunch of the same roses.

'Her shoes – such tiny little shoes to fit such tiny little feet – had high red heels, and she wore dainty white silk mittens on her small, exquisitely-shaped hands. Oh! I tell you there wasn't another girl at the dance to match Lady Green-Sleeves for looks; I knew that directly I caught sight of her bending over the wide balustrade. Besides, there was something about her that set her apart from all other women – a delicate, ineffable charm, a distinctive daintiness, a curious elusiveness. The extraordinary thing was – at least, I thought it extraordinary first of all – that no-one else seemed to see her bending over the balcony rail, for I remember turning to one of the other men of the party and asking him if he knew who Lady Green-Sleeves was, but he shook his head and looked at me queerly.

' "I don't see anyone on the balcony," he said, peering up. "It's quite deserted." And as he spoke Lady Green-Sleeves disappeared.

'I couldn't make out what in the world had become of her, how she had managed to flit away so quickly; but I caught sight of her about a quarter of an hour later standing alone and partnerless in a corner of the ballroom. The band was playing "The Choristers' Waltz", playing it well, and I thought what a shame it was that such a bewitching little lady should not be dancing – I couldn't think what all the men were about. I expect my partner, a plump, unattractive girl, dressed as a Swiss peasant, found me uncommonly dull and distrait during the rest of our waltz – I kept watching Lady Green-Sleeves, I remember. Presently I lost sight of her; she disappeared just as suddenly as she had vanished from the balcony, and I couldn't for the life of me imagine what had become of her. I determined to ask my hostess for an introduction to Lady Green-Sleeves, however; so after I had sat out with my Swiss girl, given her an ice, and handed her over thankfully to her next partner, I made my way up to Mrs Latham – for that was my hostess's name – and asked her if she would very kindly introduce me to the girl who was wearing a green silk mantle, a creamy silk petticoat, and a little white lace cap, and who did not appear to be dancing very much.

'Mrs Latham looked distinctly puzzled.

' "I am awfully sorry, Mr Vance," she answered, "but I don't seem to know the girl whom you want to be introduced to, or to recognise her from your description. It's very stupid of me, I know, but so many people have brought friends with them tonight, that perhaps I have not noticed the lady who is wearing a green silk mantle. If you can only find her, I will introduce you to her at once, with the greatest pleasure."

'I gazed helplessly round the ballroom, and as I did so I suddenly caught sight of Lady Green-Sleeves. She was standing by the raised daïs on which the band were playing; she was still alone and un-attended.

' "There she is!" I cried, turning to Mrs Latham. "There's Lady Green-Sleeves by the daïs."

'Mrs Latham looked straight across the room at Lady Green-Sleeves. As she did so her eyes opened – opened wide.

' "How extraordinary!" she exclaimed. "To think that I never caught sight of that girl before – noticed her! Why, she ought to be the belle of the ball; and she's paid us such a pretty compliment, Mr Vance; she has copied the dress of one of our ancestresses – copied it exactly. The portrait hangs in the long gallery, and now I come to think of it, she's strikingly like poor Mistress Latham's portrait – yes, there really is an extraordinary resemblance."

'Mrs Latham rose from her chair. She was a tall, dignified woman – one of those slow, quiet women whom it is impossible to hurry. I wished she would hasten her pace as she made her leisurely way round the ballroom towards the bandstand – I was so afraid that Lady Green-Sleeves would disappear again; and my fears were not ill-founded. We had to wait for a second to allow a couple who were dancing to pass us, and during that brief second lady Green-Sleeves had disappeared. When we reached the bandstand she had gone.

'Mrs Latham looked at me in a puzzled sort of way. "Dear me, Mr Vance, how very annoying," she remarked, "and how singular." I could see she looked vaguely troubled – a little bewildered.

' "It's all right, Mrs Latham," I assured her. "Don't you worry about me. I will contrive to get introduced to Lady Green-Sleeves somehow, even if I have to introduce myself, for after all it's a fancy dress ball; we are none of us ourselves tonight, our staid, decorous, conventional selves."

'Mrs Latham hesitated, then she suddenly put a hand upon my arm.

' "If you do get introduced to Lady Green-Sleeves, if you do manage to speak to her, I wish you would bring her round to me, Mr Vance; I should like to compliment her upon her dress."

' "I shall be delighted," I answered.

'Some other guest came up at that moment and claimed Mrs Latham's attention, and so set me free to go searching for Lady Green-Sleeves, but it was a long search. She was not to be found in any of the rooms given over to the sitting-out couples, neither could I discover her in the refreshment-room. When the music sounded for the next dance she did not come back to the ballroom; just as I was giving up heart, I caught sight of her bending over the gallery balustrade again. She looked a little tired, I thought, vaguely disappointed, and she was still alone.'

Aylmer Vance paused, then he suddenly turned to me.

'You can imagine how fast I ran up those wide oak stairs, can you not, Dexter? I suppose you have been in love in your time; and I don't mind confessing to you that this was a case of love at first sight on my part. I had absolutely lost my head over Lady Green-Sleeves. I might have been a callow youth of eighteen instead of a man of thirty, and my heart beat like a boy's heart – it did indeed – when Lady Green-Sleeves suddenly turned her head and looked at me when I reached the gallery; and then, without waiting for me to speak, she dropped me a formal curtsy, the most graceful, dipping, sweeping curtsy that you could imagine; she seemed to touch the floor and then to rise again in a vast billow of silk, and her voice, when she addressed me, was extraordinarily soft and sweet.

' "Your servant, sir."

'That was all she said, but the pretty conceit of the words pleased me; here was a masquerader who was clearly acting up to her part.

'I made my very best bow.

' "Will you accord me the pleasure of a dance, madam?" I requested. "I have my hostess's permission to introduce myself to you. My name is Aylmer Vance."

' "I should be delighted for you to lead me out in a dance, Mr Vance," the little lady answered, "but unfortunately I know none of these modern dances; they are after my time."

'A faint note of regret tinged Lady Green-Sleeves' voice as she spoke. The corners of her mouth drooped a little.

' "Oh! You know how to dance the waltz, madam," I protested. "It is true that it is a dance that does not accord with our costume, but still – "

'I bowed, and offered my arm, but she declined it with a faint shake of her head.

' "I am afraid I could not venture on that dance, sir. The very music to which the dancers revolve has an unfamiliar sound to me, and yet it is tuneful music – very tuneful."

' "May I have the honour of taking you in to supper? I believe supper is to be served at twelve o'clock, and it is a quarter to twelve now."

' "I never take supper, sir." Lady Green-Sleeves folded her little hands together, the little hands that I longed to hold in my own; then she suddenly looked at me from under her long lashes, her face dimpled into smiles. "You will think me vastly uncivil. I declined your invitation to dance with you and to have supper, but I'll tell you what I will do, sir; I will take you into my own parlour, and we will sit and converse there together till midnight strikes."

' "I should like nothing better," I answered; but as I said the words I felt puzzled – distinctly puzzled, for my hostess had told me that she did not know who the girl in the green mantle was, and yet Lady Green-Sleeves must be staying here – she must be one of the house-party. It was all rather mysterious, to say the least of it.

' "I will take you to my parlour at once. To confess the truth, I shall not be sorry to rest there a few minutes. I find this gay scene a little confusing, and the music is very strident."

'Lady Green-Sleeves glanced slowly about her. She appeared to be trying to remember something, then her brow suddenly cleared.

' "Ah! I recollect; this is the way to the oak parlour."

'She led me along a balcony, stopping in front of a closed door. She gazed at me silently, as though asking me to open the door.

'I obeyed that glance. I turned the handle and held the door open. Lady Green-Sleeves gave a happy little cry when she found herself in the parlour; her eyes roved round the queer little three-cornered room, a soft smile played on her lips.

' "My own parlour – I bid you welcome to it."

'She sat down on a big chair. She folded her small mittened hands in her lap; she glanced about the room with eager interest.

' "Hardly anything has been changed; the parlour is very much as I left it. The curtains have been altered, and my spinet has gone. The old mirror still hangs over the mantelpiece, however; 'tis over a hundred and fifty years since that glass reflected my face."

'I laughed – this was pretty fooling, then I gazed round the oak-panelled room in my turn. It was full of quaint old furniture; there was a beautiful apple-green tea set in a high china cupboard, a big bowl full of sweet-scented purple violets stood on a gate-leg table; the air was quite heavy with the perfume of the flowers – oppressively heavy.

' "It is so strange to come back again."

'Lady Green-Sleeves spoke in soft, reflectful tones. She seemed to have forgotten me for the moment and to be talking to herself.

' "Where have you been?" I asked. "Abroad?"

'She started and smiled – a faint, curious smile.

' "Very far away, and I found it difficult to come back – exceedingly difficult; but, indeed, I wanted to see what the world is like now-adays. I protest it has greatly changed." She gave an airy wave of her little hands. "I was so young when my time came – barely seventeen; an' 'twas hard to say farewell to this world. I would gladly have remained here longer. I was the toast of the country, and my worshipful parents made my days one long delight; but I fell into a decline suddenly."

' "Am I to understand that I am conversing with a ghost?"

'I put the question laughingly to Lady Green-Sleeves, never doubt-ing that the pretty little masquerader, as I took her to be, would laugh back; but instead of laughing she gazed at me reproachfully.

' "Why, indeed, sir, I thought you knew that. Oh! 'twas a foolish thought of mine to return to my old home tonight. This world belongs to another generation than mine, and I feel I am a stranger in my father's house – a flitting guest."

'She paused. A tear trembled on one of her long eyelashes.

' "I do not understand modern ways. Everything is unfamiliar to me – strange; and the glamour has departed. Once it would have pleased me vastly to dance till the dawn stole into the ballroom, but it would be no such great pleasure now; I have tasted deeper joys, known far more exquisite pleasures."

'She spoke with intense gravity, intense simplicity, but I still thought that Lady Green-Sleeves was playing a part. I could not believe that it was really an apparition from another world who was addressing me; but I knew one thing – I knew that I had lost my heart to the girl in the green silk mantle – lost it irretrievably.

' "Dear Lady Green-Sleeves!" I threw myself on my knees at her feet. "Now that you have come back to this world, won't you stay here – consent to remain in it? Will you be angry with me when I tell you that I have dared to fall in love with you?"

' "What! You have fallen in love with me?" She clasped her little hands tightly together; she gave the low, delighted laugh of an innocent coquette. "Oh, la! Sir, what a romance! But indeed" – her laugh was suddenly followed by a sigh, a short, sweet sigh – "I may not listen to lovers' vows; it would not be right, it would not be fair to you. My time for love is over. I told you, did I not, that I died when I was barely seventeen?"

' "Oh! Lady Green-Sleeves, Lady Green-Sleeves, don't tease me any longer by pretending to be a ghost. Don't you realise that I am speaking to you seriously – that I am in earnest? I tell you that I love you – that I have fallen in love at first sight, and I want to know your name; I want to be allowed to call you and see you, to woo you, to win you."

'She rose to her feet, her silk skirts rustling heavily, the laces fluttering at her breast, but she was not angry with me – oh, no, she was not angry.

' "Sir, believe me, I am very sorry that I have got to leave you. I wish that we had met a hundred and fifty years ago, that we could have danced together, for indeed, sir, none of the suitors who wooed me in the past took my fancy as greatly as you have done, and yet they were brave gentlemen in their day – brave gentlemen."

'She paused a second. She fixed her big blue eyes upon me. Her voice was like the sweetest and most exquisite music, but it seemed to come from a long way off.

' "This may not be farewell, sir. It is quite likely that in the future we shall meet again, but not in this world – oh, no, not in this world – indeed, it is more than likely." She hesitated. "Shall we say '*Au revoir*' instead of 'Goodbye'?"

'She swept me another of her long sweeping curtsies, and I realised that she was on the eve of taking her departure. I begged her passionately to stay with me, but she shook her head.

' "Indeed, sir, you must not ask that of me. I had a foolish fancy to come back to this world, as I told you. I remembered it as such a brave place, but now that I have returned – now that I can contrast it with another land that I know – why, I would not remain here if I could." She gave a gentle little wave of her hands. "I wish I could make you see the truth as plainly as I see it, sir. This world lacks reality, and the men and women who inhabit it are but as changing shadows; here today, they will be gone tomorrow. There is nothing in this world that endures except – except love."

'She looked at me straight in the eyes as she said the last words. I remember that I opened my arms, and would have drawn her into my embrace, only she stepped back.

' "No, sir – no!" she rebuked me. "Your lips may not touch mine any more than my lips may touch yours. Now I am going back from whence I came."

' "Where are you going?" I cried passionately. "Do you prefer the grave to my arms, Lady Green-Sleeves – to my love?"

'She shook her head.

' "The grave – what have I to do with the grave? I said farewell to my mortal body over a hundred years ago; I have merely clothed myself in my old semblance to come here. I am a spirit – an immortal spirit – and it is not to the grave I am returning, but life – life!"

'She smiled. There was such wisdom in her smile, such infinite knowledge; and then, before my eyes, she slowly faded away – vanished. I found myself alone in the oak parlour, most tragically, most sombrely alone. I could hear the violins playing wild gipsy music in the ballroom, I could hear the rhythmical swing of the dancers' feet, and "tip-tap" down the passage sounded like the click of little red-heeled shoes; but I knew – something seemed to tell me – that even if I went out on to the balcony I should not see her. I realised that no-one on this earth would ever catch a glimpse of Lady Green-Sleeves again; her home was in a better country.'

Aylmer Vance paused. He put up his hands to his eyes and he sighed – sighed heavily.

'Ah, me – it might have been! Still, it's no use to cherish foolish fancies, is it, Dexter – to dream day and night about a little sweet-eyed ghost – a little lady who will never revisit this dusty old world again. It's better to be practical and sensible – and to forget.'

I looked at him very gravely.

'You will never be able to forget her,' I said slowly, 'to really forget Lady Green-Sleeves; and you will meet her one day, Vance – you know you will.'

'How can I tell?' He shrugged his shoulders. 'It may all have been hallucination on my part; and yet Mrs Latham saw Lady Green-Sleeves too – or thought she did; but, of course, I may have conveyed the impression to her – it may only have been a case of thought transference. Still, for me Lady Green-Sleeves exists – will always exist.'

He rose slowly to his feet. He stretched himself, and stood up – a tall, lean figure in the sunshine.

'She said "*Au revoir*" – not "Goodbye", mark you; I like to remember that – that she only said "*Au revoir*".'

The Fire Unquenchable

One night Aylmer Vance handed me a book of poems in manuscript, and asked me to read it.

We had spent a quiet day fishing, wandering to quite a considerable distance from the inn, and sport had occupied us to the complete exclusion of any other subject whatever. Perhaps, in a sense, it was a healthy return to the normal.

It was as we bade each other good night that he handed me the book, producing it from one of his pockets. It was roughly bound in brown paper – merely a number of closely-written sheets fastened together – and there was no kind of title page nor any suggestion as to the name of the author. The verses were all inscribed by hand, and the writing was obviously feminine, neat and precise. That was my impression from the first casual glance.

'I don't know if you are like me,' Vance remarked, 'and care to read when you are in bed. Anyhow, I'd like you to glance through these poems – for I think you will allow they are poems in the strict sense of the word – and let me know in the morning what sort of impression you get from them.'

Vance spoke carelessly, but some instinct warned me that he had an ulterior motive in wishing me to peruse the book, and so I decided that I would read it from end to end even if I kept awake all night to do so.

We bade each other good night, and I made my way to my bed-room – a charming room, criss-crossed with old oak beams and possessing low lattice windows, just the sort of thing that one would expect in such an inn as the Magpie, which had stood just as it was for quite four hundred years. The only trace of modernity it possesses is the electric light, but this has been so artfully introduced that somehow it does not seem to strike a discordant note.

I threw one of the windows open and gazed out. It was a sultry night, characterised by alternate phases of light and darkness, as the moon either rode clear of scudding clouds or was obscured by them.

The western horizon was black and threatening. The atmosphere struck me as electric, and I thought it more than likely that a storm was gathering.

I took the book and got into bed, propping myself up comfortably against the pillows, and prepared to give my undivided attention to the subject in hand.

I don't profess to be a judge of poetry – or, indeed, of any kind of literature. Hard legal documents are more in my line. However, I hadn't read many of the stanzas in that book before I was quite convinced that this was the real thing – genuine poetry, as Vance had said.

There was something about it very difficult to describe. If it makes my meaning clear, I would say that the writer had a curious faculty of drawing quite ordinary things – say a flower, or a tree, or a human personality – in such a way that one saw that flower, or that tree, or that person, not with one's natural living eyes, but with the eyes of the spirit. One derived a curious sense of being outside one's self and of looking down upon the world from some other sphere, a sphere of infinite vastness and mystery.

But there is no need to dilate upon this subject any further, for the poems of Ewan Trail are now known to the world; they have met with the recognition that they deserve, and the curious feature which I have noticed has been commented upon over and over again.

I believe, however, that I am now giving the real story of these poems to the world for the first time.

I read steadily for an hour or more, and the sense of fatigue which had oppressed me when I went to bed, seemed to have departed altogether. My brain became unusually active and alert – indeed, it had to be so, for the handwriting that I was perusing was not always quite easy to decipher. There were curious breaks here and there, followed by blank spaces – as if inspiration had failed – and sometimes I noticed an exactly contrary effect – that is to say, the words ran into each other as if the writer had been so absorbed that the pen had not been lifted from the paper.

I must not forget to mention that before starting to read seriously, I glanced at the last page, and gathered that the manuscript was incomplete – a break had come in the middle of a poem, and there were some curious marks as if there had been an attempt to write further, but the pen had only straggled away across the page, leaving a series of indecipherable lines and curves.

Gradually, as I read, I became conscious of a remarkable sensation which, absorbed as I was, I had not noticed as soon as I might otherwise have done. It was that the atmosphere of my room had become almost insufferably hot. I found my forehead wet with perspiration. It was a dry heat, quite distinct from the warmth of the night – just as if I had a hot fire burning in my room.

I closed my eyes, though, as I have said, I didn't feel in the least bit sleepy, and tried to think it out. My whole body was tingling, the blood in my veins seemed to run like liquid fire. It occurred to me that I ought to get out of bed to investigate – perhaps the inn itself was burning – but when I tried to move I simply couldn't do so – I was like a man poisoned with curare – my senses were keenly alert, but I had lost all power over my limbs. I tried to continue reading, but there was a purple haze before my eyes – it rolled up so that all was dark and then dissipated, allowing me to see the written page of the book I was still holding – but this only for a moment, as the darkness quickly supervened again. I was reminded of the moon in its struggle to penetrate the clouds.

I lay there propped up against my pillows as if I were in a trance, and soon the purple haze before my eyes seemed to envelop everything so that I could not distinguish a single object in the room. Yet I knew that my eyes were wide open; it was just as if I was staring into illimitable space.

And first it was nothing but a deep purple void, and then, after a little while, I was conscious of shafts of fire shooting across that void – long streaks of light, like falling stars or meteors, only the word 'falling' is hardly correct, for they passed in all directions; and there were many that flew upwards like rockets, and these seemed to coalesce with those that fell, forming a glowing mass that would remain stationary for a moment or two, growing brighter and brighter until the glare was so overpowering that my eyes were unable to support it. Then the purple mantle would roll up again and darkness supervene.

And presently – it seemed so astonishingly natural to me, just as if what was happening was the rational sequence of all that had gone before – the mist gradually dispersed again – or rather, I should say, it lifted like a series of diaphanous curtains rising one after another – so that the scene behind was at first little more than a blur, giving merely a suggestion of shapes which became clearer and clearer as each curtain went up, so that at last, instead of my own room being revealed to me, which was what I had expected, my queer many-cornered room, with its dimity-covered furniture and its lattice windows and white-washed walls, all lit up by the incongruous glare of the electric light, I found myself gazing into another room altogether – a room that was absolutely unknown to me and which had no light in it save that of a red-shaded lamp.

There was an old-fashioned four-post bedstead to one side, and the bed was not, nor had been, occupied, for the sheets, turned back, were quite smooth and unruffled. The room was panelled in dark oak, and directly facing me was a large window which stood wide open, so that through it I could see the sky – or, rather, I could see an expanse of inky blackness which quivered at frequent intervals, as if it were rent by summer lightning. And somehow I felt that the heat in that room was as intolerable as it was in my own.

And through the window, in the glow of the lightning, I could clearly distinguish the swaying heads of pine trees, trees that must have been growing close up to the house, and so real was my vision that I could hear the very rustling of the wind in the branches, a queer, gentle soughing which seemed to fall upon my ears like the refrain of a long-forgotten song; and the scent of the pine was in my nostrils, too – that deep aromatic perfume always intensified when there is a storm in the air.

There was a small table drawn up by the window, and at that table sat a woman. She was writing by the light of the shaded lamp; her back was turned to me, and she was leaning forward, deeply engrossed in her work. There was a small clock on a bracket close by – I remember it particularly, for the sound of its ticking was like that of a pulsing human heart. The woman glanced at it now and again, but did not slacken in her work. She wrote on feverishly, and it seemed to me that there was something curious about the way she held her pen. Her fingers appeared to exert no pressure upon it, they merely followed its course – it was much more as if the pen, merely maintained in an upright position by her hand, was writing of its own accord.

The woman was slender, and delicately made, and she was dressed in black, and she had a wonderful aureole of golden hair which positively glowed when the lightning illuminated it. I felt that she must be wonderfully beautiful, and I was possessed of an acute longing to see her face. And presently this wish was gratified, for, uttering a low cry which fell distinctly upon my ears, she dropped her pen, pushed back her chair, and turned. It was just as if she had heard some sound behind her, and I can hardly describe the eager, expectant look upon the face that, for a moment, was turned to me.

It was, as I had guessed, a face of exceptional beauty. The woman was quite young, little more than a girl, but she seemed to have lost, if I may express it so, the natural glamour and health of youth – it was the face of one who had passed through terrible stress of soul, if not of body – a violent spiritual stress, which had caused the delicately-rounded cheeks to lose their contour, the warm colour to fade, the exquisitely-moulded lips to become bloodless, and the eyes hollow and weary. And yet those eyes! I shall carry the impression of them till I go to my own grave, for if the rest of the face was like the face of a spirit from another world, those eyes shone with the very agony of life. I don't know why I have used the word 'agony' in this connection, but it is the one that most accurately expresses my meaning – I can only repeat that the woman's eyes blazed with life – a life that was equivalent to exquisite pain.

The desire, the intense eager longing for something unattainable, for something beyond the ken of humanity – that is what I read in the sombre flame of those eyes; and I knew instinctively that when she turned it was in the hope, the wild, frantic desire, that the thing she longed for might be granted to her.

But it seemed that her desire, for the moment at least, was to go ungratified, for nothing happened, and with an expression of unutterable despair she stepped to the window, and, with arms extended, seemed to be invoking the night. And as she stood there, her arms lifted above her head, there came a flash of vivid lightning, so vivid that for a moment my eyes were dazzled and the vision was blotted out.

It lasted only the briefest second, I can swear to that, yet, when sight was restored to me, the woman was no longer alone. A man was with her – a tall, lean man, whose face was as white as her own, and whose hair was black as hers was golden. He wore some sort of cloak, and it glistened as though rain had fallen upon it; but whence he had come or how he had entered the room, I could not guess.

He clasped the woman in his arms, enveloping her, as it were, with his cloak. For a moment, however, I caught sight of her face, and if her eyes had glowed before, they were burning now as if with living fire. And I knew that her wish was gratified – that the impossible had become possible – that *He* had come. And so they stood, and no word passed between them, for had either spoken I should have been aware of it.

I was as conscious, for instance, of the low rumble of the thunder as I was of the lightning which played about them so that they seemed to stand enveloped in flame. And I could hear the ticking of the clock also.

And after a while the man, still holding the woman closely to him, stooped over the table and picked up the pen and wrote, apparently completing a sentence which the woman had left unfinished. And when this was done he laid the pen down, and instinctively I knew that there was finality in what he did and that the pen would be needed no more.

And then, over the completed manuscript, the lips of the man and woman met and hung together, and so, slowly, she clinging to him and covered by his cloak, they made their way to the door. I saw it open to allow them to pass out and then close gently behind them.

The clock struck the hour of two. The lamp burned on steadily, throwing its glare upon the completed page; then there came another blinding flash of lightning, and, with it, the vision passed.

The transition was so sudden that at first I could hardly realise that I was in my own familiar room at the Magpie Inn. I rubbed my eyes, for I felt dazed and not sure that I was fully awake. And, indeed, my experiences of the night were not yet over, for, looking towards the window, I was conscious of a curious glare, which was not that of lightning, for this, so vivid in my dream, was here but a feeble reflection of a distant storm.

But a still more pressing sensation demanded my attention. I became conscious of a sense of tingling pain in my left arm, which was lying across the open book upon my knees. 'Pain' is, perhaps, hardly the right word – my arm felt more as if it had been severely scorched by the sun; and this, I argued at first, was quite possible, since I had had my coat off and shirt sleeves turned up while fishing this afternoon.

Only, if this were so, why should it be only my left arm that was affected? I examined it and found it red from wrist to elbow, and on the underside only, while upon my right arm there was no trace of scorching whatever.

It was curious and inexplicable, as, too, was the heat in the room which had now become almost stifling. I sprang out of bed – for I had recovered the use of my limbs by now – closed the book and laid it aside, and then stepped quickly across to the open window. It was necessary to find some explanation for that persistent glow in the sky. I had a momentary fear that the inn might be on fire.

But the cause was soon quite clear. There was a fire, but it could not be less than twenty miles away – perhaps more than that. I ascribed it at once to one of those conflagrations of forest and common land, unfortunately only too frequent in some parts of Surrey. I have seen acres of wood and heather made black and desolate by their ravages.

And so this fire did not in the least explain the heat of my room. Could it be only a mental impression? I asked myself that question as I reached my hand out of the window and then stretched out my head as far as it would go. But the night air was pleasantly cool and refreshing. The heat was undoubtedly within. And so, puzzled and wondering, but overcome with fatigue, I went back to bed, switched off the light, and was soon sleeping profoundly.

In spite of my strange experiences of the night, I was up and about quite early – soon after seven, for it was at that hour that I usually had breakfast with my friend, Aylmer Vance. I found him in the comfortable parlour of the inn, and he was already half way through his morning meal, which was usually a light one.

He smiled and nodded as I took my place at his table and laid the paper-bound book down beside him.

'Well?' he inquired, lifting his eyebrows a little, and, I think, scanning my face rather curiously.

'They're wonderful poems,' I said. 'The author of them – I don't know if it is a man or a woman – should make a big reputation.'

Having regard to my vision of the night, I had come to the conclusion that the author was a woman; I was surprised, therefore, when Vance replied:

'The author is a man – Ewan Trail – and if he makes a reputation, as I am sure he will, it will be a posthumous one. For he died only a few months ago, a bitterly disappointed man. He died tragically.

Presently you shall hear the story. But first I want you to tell me any impressions you may have received while reading the poems. Don't be afraid of mentioning anything, however slight – I have a reason for asking you.'

So I had guessed correctly that Vance wished to put me to the test, and I wondered, as I had been wondering ever since I got up that morning, if my vision of the night and the heat and the other incidents had any real significance. I felt more than a little agitated, for this was my first experience of anything in the remotest degree concerned with the occult.

I had been doing justice to an excellent dish of eggs and bacon, but now I laid down my knife and fork.

'I don't know if you will call it an impression,' I faltered, 'but the most remarkable sensation I experienced last night was one of intense heat. I know the weather was hot and that there was a storm, but it wasn't like the natural heat of the atmosphere – '

'More like that of a fire?' Vance interrupted.

I nodded. 'Yes; that of an intensely hot fire. My forehead was bathed with perspiration; and look here, Vance' – I lifted my arm and pulled up my sleeve – 'how do you account for this? I thought of sunburn, but it's only the one arm, and on the underside of it.'

'Curious,' he muttered, 'very interesting. In what position did you hold your arm last night?'

'It was resting upon the book,' I replied, casting a side glance at that apparently innocent object, which still lay upon the table where I had placed it. 'And I had a sort of a vision,' I resumed in a low, almost awestruck tone, 'while I was sitting propped up in bed with my arm upon the book. It may have been a dream, just an ordinary dream – but I've never had such a dream before.'

'Tell me about it.' Vance leaned forward, his elbows upon the table, his chin supported by his hands. His keen eyes were fixed upon me; he appeared intensely interested.

I told him of my vision, omitting not the smallest detail. It had impressed itself so vividly upon my mind that I forgot nothing. Vance sat quite still, not interrupting me once.

'This is most deeply interesting, Dexter,' he said when I had concluded; 'and what is more, it goes to show that you – you yourself – are possessed of powers which probably you have never dreamed of.' His lips parted in a slight smile. 'I suppose, a few days ago, you would have been consumed with amusement if anyone had suggested that you, a hard-headed man of the law, had it in you to be a clairvoyant, a medium – and yet such is undoubtedly the case, and it was because I suspected it that I gave you those poems to read. And now I know this, Dexter, I hope that we may do good work together, you and I – work for the furtherance of human knowledge in the little-known paths of what we now call the super-physical, but which may prove to be the normal and natural after all.'

He extended his long slim hand to me across the table, and I took it, not without a certain trepidation and bewilderment, for all this was so astonishingly new to me, so absolutely unexpected. It was true that I had never realised the latent gifts of which, apparently, I was possessed. And the wonder of it all was great upon me.

'You think,' I faltered, 'that my dream – my vision – had actual significance?'

'I have no doubt about it,' was the reply. 'You were most certainly in telepathic rapport last night with someone with whom I am acquainted. What the vision actually portends it is difficult to say. I have my fears, but we shall know the truth quite soon – this very morning.'

I drew a deep breath and accepted my destiny. Luckily, being of independent means, my profession had never meant more to me than the occupation which every man should have. And now I had found a fresh occupation – one to which I could give myself up with earnest devotion. From that day forth I was a disciple of Aylmer Vance.

'There is one fact that I should mention,' I said, when he had smilingly agreed that we should in future make common cause, 'and that is that there really was a fire last night. I saw it from my window, and I think it had not long broken out; but it was spreading rapidly – a forest fire, I am practically certain. But it was a long way off – quite twenty miles, I calculated – and so, of course, it is absurd to think that I could have felt the heat of it.'

Vance rose to his feet as I spoke. A look of agitation had come into his face.

'A forest fire?' he questioned. 'Tell me in what direction it was.'

'My room faces the north-west.'

He made a rapid mental calculation. 'To the north-west, and about twenty miles away. Dexter' – he spoke hurriedly – 'we mustn't delay. This may be of deep importance.'

He rang the bell, and when the servant came gave instructions that his car should be brought round at once. Then he turned to me.

'Williams shall drive us,' he said. Williams was his chauffeur. 'That will leave me free to tell you all there is to be told as we go along. Will you be ready to start in a few minutes?'

Barely a quarter of an hour later we were on our way to some destination with which I was still unacquainted. Vance's car was a Darracq, light and swift. He usually drove it himself, but on this occasion he had delegated that duty to his man. It was in order that he might tell me a story, and here, more or less in his words, is the story he told.

'Early in the spring of this year I was invited by a man with whom I had a slight acquaintance – a Mr Tyrrell – to spend a few days with him at his country house and investigate certain curious happenings. The house is named "Cheswold Lodge", and it is situated near the little village of Hillinghurst, which is at the foot of the south slope of the Hog's Back. It is there we are going.

'I had travelled down by train to Guildford, where Tyrrell met me with his car, and he told me about the trouble as we drove to his house – just as I am telling it to you now. He had only been in residence at Cheswold Lodge – he and his wife and their two little girls – for about a month, and curious things had happened almost at once.

'In a sense, he had bought the house out of charity. A tragedy had happened there the preceding winter, and people were inclined to look upon it askance. It is an old house – as you will see – and it had belonged for generations to the family of the Trails, the last representative of which was Ewan Trail, who is the author of the poems which you have just read.

'Now Ewan was a rather extraordinary individual – the "mad poet" he used to be called in the neighbourhood. He was a tall, lean fellow, with a face that was almost mediaeval in character, very black hair, and a complexion that was as olive as that of a southerner. I expect he had foreign blood in him somewhere.'

Here I ventured on an interruption. I could scarcely help myself. 'Was it he whom I saw last night?' I asked in an awed whisper.

'You shall judge for yourself as I proceed,' responded Vance. Then he took up his story again. 'Ewan Trail was so much of a poet that he could not get on with ordinary people, and he was really quite incapable of managing his own affairs. He had started life with good prospects and a fair fortune, but somehow he contrived to fritter practically everything away. His one absorbing idea was that his poems should be given to the world – that the genius which he knew he possessed should not be overlooked, should not go down with him unrecognised to the grave.

'And he knew that he had not very long to live. He was endowed with a fine appreciation of the beauty of life, and yet the spirit from which he had derived his inspiration was housed in a weak and diseased body, although that, too, had a certain beauty of its own.

'About a year ago he married, and took his wife to live with him at Cheswold Lodge. She adored him passionately – indeed, the passion was mutual – but it was essentially a passion of the spirit. For Leila Trail, like her husband, held but a poor tenure upon life. She was very young and very beautiful, and many of Trail's finest poems are addressed to her.

'Well, disaster fell upon them quite soon after their marriage. Ewan Trail lost practically all his money; but this, at the time, seemed to be of but small account to him, for he believed that he had only to publish his poems and that all the world would be at his feet. It was not for himself, however, that he cared so much – he did not mind poverty, if you understand me – but it was for his poetry, that those verses of his, those rhapsodies of emotion, the passionate expression of his soul, should live when he was dust. The fire that was in him, that was, in fact, consuming him, must have its vent.

'And then began a series of the most bitter disappointments. For, strange as it may seem to you who have read his poems, there wasn't a publisher in London who would take the risk of producing them. Poetry, they said, was a drug upon the market and, except in the case of one or two famous names, not worth looking at. Who would purchase a book of verses by Ewan Trail, whose name had never been heard of? If he chose, he might, of course, be his own publisher. But here a fatal difficulty arose – Trail had no money, absolutely no money, that he might expend in such a way. His creditors were already pressing him on every side.

'And so, like Chatterton before him, and others whom one may think of even at a quite recent date, Trail, who was barely twenty-five years of age, took his own life. He shot himself in a little summer-house situated in the midst of the pine wood which reached almost up to the very walls of Cheswold Lodge, and which stretches out thence for the best part of a mile towards the south until it merges in open common land.

'Poor Leila was left destitute. The house and everything it contained would have been sold up had not my friend Tyrrell, who was acquainted with her family, come to the rescue. He purchased the house as it stood, and he invited Leila to remain with him as governess to his two little girls. She is there now, Dexter – at least, she was there yesterday. But now I'm not so sure – I'm not so sure.'

Vance paused in his story, and the pause was impressive. We were nearing our destination by now, for, straight ahead of us, I recognised the long unbroken ridge of the Hog's Back. We were following a road that undulated across open country, and the air was fragrant with the scent of heather.

Presently Vance resumed. 'Having told me all this about the former owner of his house, Tyrrell proceeded to recount his troubles since he had entered into occupation. They were of a curious character, and new to me, in spite of all my experience.

'The danger with which he had to contend was, in a sense, a material one – the danger of fire.

'There had been several outbreaks in the house itself, all of which were wholly inexplicable. Two or three had occurred in the bedroom which Trail and his wife had occupied, and which Leila had been allowed to retain for her own use. Once it was curtains in front of the window, another time the curtains of the bed, and then again fire had been discovered springing up mysteriously from underneath an easy chair which had been a particular favourite of the dead poet's. Luckily, all these outbreaks were discovered in time to prevent any serious damage being done.

'In other parts of the house, too, the same thing had occurred, and especially in Trail's study, which Tyrrell, who was also a literary man by profession, had now adapted to his own purpose.

'"Do you know, Vance," so Tyrrell said to me, "there was one occasion at least when I actually saw the fire break out, and there was no possible cause for it, no suggestion of carelessness on my part or upon that of anyone else. I'd been sitting up late to finish an article that I was writing, and everyone had gone to bed. There was a fire burning in the grate, for it was early in the year, and the nights were cold. The only other light in the room was from a couple of lamps, one of which was on the table where I was working, a shaded reading-lamp; and the other, a tall standard, was at some distance away. I'm not a smoker, so there can be no suggestion of a dropped match or anything of that sort. Well, the room seemed to me to get hotter and hotter – and it wasn't at all the first time that I had noticed the peculiar heat, for one experienced it all over the house – nearly every member of my family had noticed it as well, and so had the servants – and by degrees this heat became so intolerable that I got up to throw open the window. And then – well, I'm not a superstitious man, and I've never in my life before had anything to do with the superphysical – the queerest sensation you can imagine went through me, and I felt a conviction that I wasn't alone in the room. I'd had the same sort of feeling on other occasions – the involuntary glance over one's shoulder to assure one's self that there was no-one there – I expect you know what I mean. But upon this occasion I felt positively sure, and when I looked towards the chair upon which I had been sitting, I give you my word that a cold shudder went through me, for though I couldn't distinguish anything – anything definite, that is to say – I somehow knew in my inner conscience that the chair was occupied. And then, almost immediately afterwards, I smelt fire, and I saw smoke issuing from a drawer of the table, a drawer in which I kept my papers and which, no doubt, had served the same purpose for my predecessor. Of course, I hadn't the smallest difficulty in putting the fire out, and no material damage was done. But I cite this as an example of the sort of thing that is happening, and which is so inexplicable – and dangerous – for who can say that one day we may not be caught off our guard and have the whole place burnt down over our heads?"

'Tyrrell spoke the last words very seriously, and I had to agree with him that the danger was one not to be ignored.

'But it wasn't only in the house that these outbreaks of fire occurred. They were far more frequent in the pine wood which I have already mentioned – yet it wasn't at all the time of year when one would expect such conflagrations. Mr Tyrrell assured me that there were dozens of places in the wood where charred traces could be seen of the beginning of such fires – just as if the gipsies had been encamped there – that was the expression he used – only it was known that there had been no gipsies at that time in the neighbourhood.

'And now people were beginning to talk about it, and all sorts of stories were going round. It was said that lights were seen in the wood, like moving lanterns, and sometimes the appearances were much more erratic – someone had spoken of shooting stars, or of fireworks let off among the trees. Someone else had a yarn about a ball of fire hovering over the tree-tops and then bursting. Anyhow, the whole place had acquired a bad name.'

Here Vance paused again and then proceeded, with as much detail as time allowed, to narrate the investigations he had made into the phenomena and the conclusion to which he had arrived.

'I did not at first associate the dead poet with the mischief,' he admitted. 'I thought of a fire elemental, but quickly had to exclude that supposition. I soon assured myself, for instance, that the fires were not kindled in any spirit of mischief.'

'What, then?' I inquired. I admit I was puzzled.

'I want you to draw your own conclusions,' said Vance, 'from what I tell you. And understand that in these matters one cannot, one must not, dare to speak with certainty. Our knowledge is too vague, too indefinite.'

'You made some important discovery?'

'I made a discovery that at least indicated to me how I should act. It resulted from a careful examination of the wood, which, by the way, was regularly patrolled during the daytime – they wouldn't stay at night – by a number of boy scouts whom Tyrrell had engaged to put out any fires which they might come across. One of these boys, a particularly intelligent one, reported to me that on two or three occasions he had found pieces of burning paper in different parts of the wood, and that these, if let alone, would no doubt have given rise to more serious outbreaks. Well, at last I myself found one of these pieces of burning paper, and having extinguished it, I noticed that it bore traces of handwriting, which Leila Trail, on being consulted, recognised and was able to account for.

'She burst into a passion of tears. "I can tell you," she cried, "how that paper came to be in the wood. When Ewan's work came back to him from the publishers – when he lost all hope – he destroyed all his typewritten copies – he threw them into the fire here in the house – but his own original manuscript – the words that he had written down as they came hot from his brain – that he carried about on his own person." She lowered her voice, speaking in a tone that was charged with the deepest pain. "It was on the day that he killed himself. He was more than half distracted – I tried to pacify him, but he would not listen to me. He threw me roughly away from him – he who loved me so devotedly – and he ran off into the wood, ran wildly towards the summer-house. And I followed him as best I was able, but I could not catch him up. It was night, and there was only a dim moon, but I saw him, as he ran, tearing the manuscript of his poems into fragments and scattering them about him to the right and to the left. He destroyed everything – everything. I caught my foot in the root of a tree and fell, and I hurt myself and could not move. I lay there, crying and moaning; and I heard the report of the pistol when he shot himself, and could do nothing to prevent it – nothing."

'She broke off, sobbing as if her heart would break. I must tell you, Dexter, that I had already taken particular notice of Leila Trail, and that I had recognised the deep spirituality of her nature.

'Well, I got as many of these fragments of paper together as I could collect, and studied them. With the help of Leila, I even succeeded in reconstructing a complete poem, and though I don't profess to be an expert, I realised the worth of the thing. In any case, I came to a decided conclusion, and determined upon a course of action.

'It was Leila Trail who was to help me, and I couldn't possibly have had a better subject to deal with. As I have told you, there were times when she seemed far more spiritual than human.

'By my instruction, she sat at a table in her bedroom with the window open, and I put paper before her and a pen in her hand, and I told her to concentrate her thoughts upon her husband, to let her mind be a blank upon all other subjects. And she was wonderfully responsive; she understood what I wanted of her almost without any explanation at all.

' "If only he would come back to me," she sighed. "If only I could see him again! I love him so – I love him so!"

'You understand what I wanted of her, Dexter? You are beginning to see light, are you not? The unfortunate poet, Ewan Trail, had destroyed all his manuscript – there was no longer any possibility of giving to the world those burning and impassioned words of his. And who can say that the fire of inspiration dies with the death of the body? Who can say that, released from fleshly bonds, it does not continue to burn with a zest and ardour that we poor humans are totally unable to appreciate? I don't know; we can't really explain these things; and I myself, today, can only be said to have faintly touched the border line of understanding.

'At any rate, Dexter, you understand the supposition upon which I decided to act. If those lost poems could be regained – if, eventually, they could be given to the world – was it not possible that these pent-up fires would find their desired outlet? The fire unquenchable – the fire of inspiration – it was with that, I argued, that I had to deal.

'I have said that Leila Trail was responsive. She had never before tried her hand at automatic writing, and so it was a day or two before actual results were achieved. But when they once began it was aston-ishing – astonishing – to watch the rate with which her pen would fly across the paper. You have seen the result for yourself, for the book you were reading last night was written, every word of it, by Leila Trail under the inspiration of her dead husband. Through her he has sent his message to the world, and unless I'm very much mistaken, when those poems see the light of publicity – as they will do, for I myself shall have them published – the fire that emanates from the restless spirit of Ewan Trail, the checked flame of inspiration, will be drawn to its natural channel, where it may burn for ever, a power for good, unquenched and unquenchable in the minds and hearts of men.'

I drew a deep breath. 'Then what I saw last night – ' I ventured.

'We shall know the significance of your vision very shortly now,' he replied gravely. 'For the moment all that I feel sure of is that Ewan Trail has imparted his last message, and that he is content. You noticed, of course, that the book I gave you is incomplete. I was waiting only for the conclusion of the last poem – and I think we have that now.'

Suddenly he stood up in the car and pointed. 'Look, Dexter, look!' he exclaimed.

I looked and saw a blackened track of land where the fire had passed. The flames were not yet fully extinguished, and there were men at work tearing up the heather to prevent their further encroachment.

'You were right, Dexter,' muttered Vance; 'you saw truly. The whole wood has been destroyed. And look, Dexter, there is the house. Thank heaven, that seems to have been spared.'

Presently the car drove up to the door of Cheswold Lodge, a long, low, old-fashioned building of many gables. Mr Tyrrell arrived almost at the same time as ourselves – he had been assisting his men with their work in the burning wood. His face, I noticed, was very grave, and he hardly waited to be introduced to me, so anxious did he seem to impart some important intelligence to my friend. And instinctively I knew what that intelligence must be.

'You may speak without reserve, Tyrrell,' said Vance. 'Mr Dexter is fully acquainted with all the circumstances of the case.'

And so Mr Tyrrell told his story. Leila Trail was dead. She had been found lying in the same summer-house where her husband had met his death, and there was no sign of injury upon the body, and she looked very happy, happier far than she had done in life. The fire had swept round the summer-house, which stood in a clear space, and had left it absolutely untouched.

What was the cause of the fire? No doubt the storm – a tree struck by lightning. So the neighbourhood decided, and there was no reason to doubt the verdict.

A little later we went together to the bedroom where Leila had been sitting overnight with her work. I recognised it at once, for every detail was as I had seen it in my vision. The lamp, extinguished now, stood on the table, and beneath it was the paper upon which she had been writing. The pen lay there where it was dropped, and the small clock upon the bracket had stopped at the hour of two.

'Look, Dexter,' said Vance simply. He pointed to the written page.

Beneath the completed poem one word had been added, and it was in quite a different handwriting to that of Leila Trail – a firm masculine handwriting. The word was 'Finis'.

And yet, perhaps, for him and for her the finish meant the real beginning.

The Vampire

Aylmer Vance had rooms in Dover Street, Piccadilly, and now that I had decided to follow in his footsteps and to accept him as my instructor in matters psychic, I found it convenient to lodge in the same house. Aylmer and I quickly became close friends, and he showed me how to develop that faculty of clairvoyance which I had possessed without being aware of it. And I may say at once that this particular faculty of mine proved of service on several important occasions.

At the same time I made myself useful to Vance in other ways, not the least of which was that of acting as recorder of his many strange adventures. For himself, he never cared much about publicity, and it was some time before I could persuade him, in the interests of science, to allow me to give any detailed account of his experiences to the world.

The incidents which I will now relate occurred very soon after we had taken up our residence together, and while I was still, so to speak, a novice.

It was about ten o'clock in the morning that a visitor was announced. He sent up a card which bore upon it the name of Paul Davenant.

The name was familiar to me, and I wondered if this could be the same Mr Davenant who was so well known for his polo playing and for his success as an amateur rider, especially over the hurdles? He was a young man of wealth and position, and I recollected that he had married, about a year ago, a girl who was reckoned the greatest beauty of the season. All the illustrated papers had given their portraits at the time, and I remember thinking what a remarkably handsome couple they made.

Mr Davenant was ushered in, and at first I was uncertain as to whether this could be the individual whom I had in mind, so wan and pale and ill did he appear. A finely-built, upstanding man at the time of his marriage, he had now acquired a languid droop of the shoulders and a shuffling gait, while his face, especially about the lips, was bloodless to an alarming degree.

And yet it was the same man, for behind all this I could recognise the shadow of the good looks that had once distinguished Paul Davenant.

He took the chair which Aylmer offered him – after the usual preliminary civilities had been exchanged – and then glanced doubtfully in my direction. 'I wish to consult you privately, Mr Vance,' he said. 'The matter is of considerable importance to myself, and, if I may say so, of a somewhat delicate nature.'

Of course I rose immediately to withdraw from the room, but Vance laid his hand upon my arm.

'If the matter is connected with research in my particular line, Mr Davenant,' he said, 'if there is any investigation you wish me to take up on your behalf, I shall be glad if you will include Mr Dexter in your confidence. Mr Dexter assists me in my work. But, of course – '

'Oh, no,' interrupted the other, 'if that is the case, pray let Mr Dexter remain. I think,' he added, glancing at me with a friendly smile, 'that you are an Oxford man, are you not, Mr Dexter? It was before my time, but I have heard of your name in connection with the river. You rowed at Henley, unless I am very much mistaken.'

I admitted the fact, with a pleasurable sensation of pride. I was very keen upon rowing in those days, and a man's prowess at school and college always remains dear to his heart.

After this we quickly became on friendly terms, and Paul Davenant proceeded to take Aylmer and myself into his confidence.

He began by calling attention to his personal appearance. 'You would hardly recognise me for the same man I was a year ago,' he said. 'I've been losing flesh steadily for the last six months. I came up from Scotland about a week ago, to consult a London doctor. I've seen two – in fact they've held a sort of consultation over me – but the result, I may say, is far from satisfactory. They don't seem to know what is really the matter with me.'

'Anaemia – heart,' suggested Vance. He was scrutinising his visitor keenly, and yet without any particular appearance of doing so. 'I believe it not infrequently happens that you athletes overdo yourselves – put too much strain upon the heart – '

'My heart is quite sound,' responded Davenant. 'Physically it is in perfect condition. The trouble seems to be that it hasn't enough blood to pump into my veins. The doctors wanted to know if I had met with an accident involving a great loss of blood – but I haven't.

I've had no accident at all, and as for anaemia, well I don't seem to show the ordinary symptoms of it. The inexplicable thing is that I've lost blood without knowing it, and apparently this has been going on for some time, for I've been getting steadily worse. It was almost imperceptible at first – not a sudden collapse, you understand, but a gradual failure of health.'

'I wonder,' remarked Vance slowly, 'what induced you to consult me? For you know, of course, the direction in which I pursue my investigations. May I ask if you have reason to consider that your state of health is due to some cause which we may describe as super-physical?'

A slight colour came to Davenant's cheeks.

'There are curious circumstances,' he said, in a low and earnest tone of voice. 'I've been turning them over in my mind, trying to see light through them. I daresay it's all the sheerest folly – and I must tell you that I'm not in the least a superstitious sort of man. I don't mean to say that I'm absolutely incredulous, but I've never given thought to such things – I've led too active a life. But, as I have said, there are curious circumstances about my case, and that is why I decided upon consulting you.'

'Will you tell me everything without reserve?' said Vance. I could see that he was interested. He was sitting up in his chair, his feet supported on a stool, his elbows on his knees, his chin in his hands – a favourite attitude of his. 'Have you,' he suggested slowly, 'any mark upon your body, anything that you might associate, however remotely, with your present weakness and ill-health?'

'It's a curious thing that you should ask me that question,' returned Davenant, 'because I have got a curious mark, a sort of scar, that I can't account for. But I showed it to the doctors, and they assured me that it could have nothing whatever to do with my condition. In any case, if it had, it was something altogether outside their experience. I think they imagined it to be nothing more than a birthmark, a sort of mole, for they asked me if I'd had it all my life. But that I can swear I haven't. I only noticed it for the first time about six months ago, when my health began to fail. But you can see for yourself.'

He loosened his collar and bared his throat. Vance rose and made a careful scrutiny of the suspicious mark. It was situated a very little to the left of the central line, just above the clavicle, and, as Vance pointed out, directly over the big vessels of the throat. My friend called to me so that I might examine it, too. Whatever the opinion of the doctors may have been, Aylmer was obviously deeply interested.

And yet there was very little to show. The skin was quite intact, and there was no sign of inflammation. There were two red marks, about an inch apart, each of which was inclined to be crescent in shape. They were more visible than they might otherwise have been owing to the peculiar whiteness of Davenant's skin.

'It can't be anything of importance,' said Davenant, with a slightly uneasy laugh. 'I'm inclined to think the marks are dying away.'

'Have you ever noticed them more inflamed than they are at present?' inquired Vance. 'If so, was it at any special time?'

Davenant reflected. 'Yes,' he replied slowly, 'there have been times, usually, I think perhaps invariably, when I wake up in the morning, that I've noticed them larger and more angry looking. And I've felt a slight sensation of pain – a tingling – oh, very slight, and I've never worried about it. Only now you suggest it to my mind, I believe that those same mornings I have felt particularly tired and done up – a sensation of lassitude absolutely unusual to me. And once, Mr Vance, I remember quite distinctly that there was a stain of blood close to the mark. I didn't think anything of it at the time, and just wiped it away.'

'I see.' Aylmer Vance resumed his seat and invited his visitor to do the same. 'And now,' he resumed, 'you said, Mr Davenant, that there are certain peculiar circumstances you wish to acquaint me with. Will you do so?'

And so Davenant readjusted his collar and proceeded to tell his story. I will tell it as far as I can, without any reference to the occasional interruptions of Vance and myself.

Paul Davenant, as I have said, was a man of wealth and position, and so, in every sense of the word, he was a suitable husband for Miss Jessica MacThane, the young lady who eventually became his wife. Before coming to the incidents attending his loss of health, he had a great deal to recount about Miss MacThane and her family history.

She was of Scottish descent, and although she had certain characteristic features of her race, she was not really Scotch in appearance. Hers was the beauty of the far South rather than that of the Highlands from which she had her origin. Names are not always suited to their owners, and Miss MacThane's was peculiarly inappropriate. She had, in fact, been christened Jessica in a sort of pathetic effort to counteract her obvious departure from normal type. There was a reason for this which we were soon to learn.

Miss MacThane was especially remarkable for her wonderful red hair, hair such as one hardly ever sees outside Italy – not the Celtic red – and it was so long that it reached to her feet, and it had an extraordinary gloss upon it, so that it seemed almost to have individual life of its own. Then she had just the complexion that one would expect with such hair, the purest ivory white, and not in the least marred by freckles, as is so often the case with red-haired girls. Her beauty was derived from an ancestress who had been brought to Scotland from some foreign shore – no-one knew exactly whence.

Davenant fell in love with her almost at once, and he had every reason to believe, in spite of her many admirers, that his love was returned. At this time he knew very little about her personal history. He was aware only that she was very wealthy in her own right, an orphan, and the last representative of a race that had once been famous in the annals of history – or rather infamous, for the Mac-Thanes had distinguished themselves more by cruelty and lust of blood than by deeds of chivalry. A clan of turbulent robbers in the past, they had helped to add many a blood-stained page to the history of their country.

Jessica had lived with her father, who owned a house in London, until his death when she was about fifteen years of age. Her mother had died in Scotland when Jessica was still a tiny child. Mr Mac-Thane had been so affected by his wife's death that, with his little daughter, he had abandoned his Scotch estate altogether – or so it was believed – leaving it to the management of a bailiff – though, indeed, there was but little work for the bailiff to do, since there were practically no tenants left. Blackwick Castle had borne for many years a most unenviable reputation.

After the death of her father, Miss MacThane had gone to live with a certain Mrs Meredith, who was a connection of her mother's – on her father's side she had not a single relation left. Jessica was absolutely the last of a clan once so extensive that intermarriage had been a tradition of the family, but which for the last two hundred years had been gradually dwindling to extinction.

Mrs Meredith took Jessica into Society – which would never have been her privilege had Mr MacThane lived, for he was a moody, self-absorbed man, and prematurely old – one who seemed worn down by the weight of a great grief.

Well, I have said that Paul Davenant quickly fell in love with Jessica, and it was not long before he proposed for her hand. To his great surprise, for he had good reason to believe that she cared for him, he met with a refusal; nor would she give any explanation, though she burst into a flood of pitiful tears.

Bewildered and bitterly disappointed, he consulted Mrs Meredith, with whom he happened to be on friendly terms, and from her he learnt that Jessica had already had several proposals, all from quite desirable men, but that one after another had been rejected.

Paul consoled himself with the reflection that perhaps Jessica did not love them, whereas he was quite sure that she cared for himself. Under these circumstances he determined to try again.

He did so, and with better result. Jessica admitted her love, but at the same time she repeated that she could not marry him. Love and marriage were not for her. Then, to his utter amaze, she declared that she had been born under a curse – a curse which sooner or later was bound to show itself in her, and which, moreover, must react cruelly, perhaps fatally, upon anyone with whom she linked her life. How could she allow a man she loved to take such a risk? Above all, since the evil was hereditary, there was one point upon which she had quite made up her mind: no child should ever call her mother – she must be the last of her race indeed.

Of course, Davenant was amazed, and inclined to think that Jessica had got some absurd idea into her head which a little reasoning on his part would dispel. There was only one other possible explanation. Was it lunacy she was afraid of?

But Jessica shook her head. She did not know of any lunacy in her family. The ill was deeper, more subtle than that. And then she told him all that she knew.

The curse – she made use of that word for want of a better – was attached to the ancient race from which she had her origin. Her father had suffered from it, and his father and grandfather before him. All three had taken to themselves young wives who had died mysteriously, of some wasting disease, within a few years. Had they observed the ancient family tradition of intermarriage this might possibly not have happened, but in their case, since the family was so near extinction, this had not been possible.

For the curse – or whatever it was – did not kill those who bore the name of MacThane. It only rendered them a danger to others. It was as if they absorbed from the blood-soaked walls of their fatal castle a deadly taint which reacted terribly upon those with whom they were brought into contact, especially their nearest and dearest.

'Do you know what my father said we have it in us to become?' said Jessica with a shudder. 'He used the word vampires. Paul, think of it – vampires – preying upon the life-blood of others.'

And then, when Davenant was inclined to laugh, she checked him. 'No,' she cried out, 'it is not impossible. Think. We are a decadent race. From the earliest times our history has been marked by bloodshed and cruelty. The walls of Blackwick Castle are impregnated with evil – every stone could tell its tale of violence, pain, lust, and murder. What can one expect of those who have spent their lifetime between its walls?'

'But you have not done so,' exclaimed Paul. 'You have been spared that, Jessica. You were taken away after your mother died, and you have no recollection of Blackwick Castle, none at all. And you need never set foot in it again.'

'I'm afraid the evil is in my blood,' she replied sadly, 'although I am unconscious of it now. And as for not returning to Blackwick – I'm not sure that I can help myself. At least, that is what my father warned me of. He said that there is something there, some compelling force, that will call me to it in spite of myself. But, oh, I don't know – I don't know, and that is what makes it so difficult. If I could only believe that all this is nothing but an idle superstition, I might be happy again, for I have it in me to enjoy life, and I'm young, very young; but my father told me these things when he was on his deathbed.' She added the last words in a low, awe-stricken tone.

Paul pressed her to tell him all that she knew, and eventually she revealed another fragment of family history which seemed to have some bearing upon the case. It dealt with her own astonishing likeness to that ancestress of a couple of hundred years ago, whose existence seemed to have presaged the gradual downfall of the clan of the MacThanes.

A certain Robert MacThane, departing from the traditions of his family, which demanded that he should not marry outside his clan, brought home a wife from foreign shores, a woman of wonderful beauty, who was possessed of glowing masses of red hair and a complexion of ivory whiteness – such as had more or less distinguished since then every female of the race born in the direct line.

It was not long before this woman came to be regarded in the neighbourhood as a witch. Queer stories were circulated abroad as to her doings, and the reputation of Blackwick Castle became worse than ever before.

And then one day she disappeared. Robert MacThane had been absent upon some business for twenty-four hours, and it was upon his return that he found her gone. The neighbourhood was searched, but without avail, and then Robert, who was a violent man and who had adored his foreign wife, called together certain of his tenants whom he suspected, rightly or wrongly, of foul play, and had them murdered in cold blood. Murder was easy in those days, yet such an outcry was raised that Robert had to take flight, leaving his two children in the care of their nurse, and for a long while Blackwick Castle was without a master.

But its evil reputation persisted. It was said that Zaida, the witch, though dead, still made her presence felt. Many children of the tenantry and young people of the neighbourhood sickened and died – possibly of quite natural causes; but this did not prevent a mantle of terror settling upon the countryside, for it was said that Zaida had been seen – a pale woman clad in white – flitting about the cottages at night, and where she passed sickness and death were sure to supervene.

And from that time the fortune of the family gradually declined. Heir succeeded heir, but no sooner was he installed at Blackwick Castle than his nature, whatever it may previously have been, seemed to undergo a change. It was as if he absorbed into himself all the weight of evil that had stained his family name – as if he did, indeed, become a vampire, bringing blight upon any not directly connected with his own house.

And so, by degrees, Blackwick was deserted of its tenantry. The land around it was left uncultivated – the farms stood empty. This had persisted to the present day, for the superstitious peasantry still told their tales of the mysterious white woman who hovered about the neighbourhood, and whose appearance betokened death – and possibly worse than death.

And yet it seemed that the last representatives of the MacThanes could not desert their ancestral home. Riches they had, sufficient to live happily upon elsewhere, but, drawn by some power they could not contend against, they had preferred to spend their lives in the solitude of the now half-ruined castle, shunned by their neighbours, feared and execrated by the few tenants that still clung to their soil.

So it had been with Jessica's grandfather and great-grandfather. Each of them had married a young wife, and in each case their love story had been all too brief. The vampire spirit was still abroad, expressing itself – or so it seemed – through the living represent-atives of bygone generations of evil, and young blood had been demanded at the sacrifice.

And to them had succeeded Jessica's father. He had not profited by their example, but had followed directly in their footsteps. And the same fate had befallen the wife whom he passionately adored. She had died of pernicious anaemia – so the doctors said – but he had regarded himself as her murderer.

But, unlike his predecessors, he had torn himself away from Blackwick – and this for the sake of his child. Unknown to her, however, he had returned year after year, for there were times when the passionate longing for the gloomy, mysterious halls and corridors of the old castle, for the wild stretches of moorland, and the dark pine woods, would come upon him too strongly to be resisted. And so he knew that for his daughter, as for himself, there was no escape, and he warned her, when the relief of death was at last granted to him, of what her fate must be.

This was the tale that Jessica told the man who wished to make her his wife, and he made light of it, as such a man would, regarding it all as foolish superstition, the delusion of a mind overwrought. And at last – perhaps it was not very difficult, for she loved him with all her heart and soul – he succeeded in inducing Jessica to think as he did, to banish morbid ideas, as he called them, from her brain, and to consent to marry him at an early date.

'I'll take any risk you like,' he declared. 'I'll even go and live at Blackwick if you should desire it. To think of you, my lovely Jessica, a vampire! Why, I never heard such nonsense in my life.'

'Father said I'm very like Zaida, the witch,' she protested, but he silenced her with a kiss.

And so they were married and spent their honeymoon abroad, and in the autumn Paul accepted an invitation to a house party in Scotland for the grouse shooting, a sport to which he was absolutely devoted, and Jessica agreed with him that there was no reason why he should forego his pleasure.

Perhaps it was an unwise thing to do, to venture to Scotland, but by this time the young couple, more deeply in love with each other than ever, had got quite over their fears. Jessica was redolent with health and spirits, and more than once she declared that if they should be anywhere in the neighbourhood of Blackwick she would like to see the old castle out of curiosity, and just to show how absolutely she had got over the foolish terrors that used to assail her.

This seemed to Paul to be quite a wise plan, and so one day, since they were actually staying at no great distance, they motored over to Blackwick, and finding the bailiff, got him to show them over the castle.

It was a great castellated pile, grey with age, and in places falling into ruin. It stood on a steep hillside, with the rock of which it seemed to form part, and on one side of it there was a precipitous drop to a mountain stream a hundred feet below. The robber Mac-Thanes of the old days could not have desired a better stronghold.

At the back, climbing up the mountain side, were dark pine woods, from which, here and there, rugged crags protruded, and these were fantastically shaped, some like gigantic and misshapen human forms, which stood up as if they mounted guard over the castle and the narrow gorge, by which alone it could be approached.

This gorge was always full of weird, uncanny sound. It might have been a storehouse for the wind, which, even on calm days, rushed up and down as if seeking an escape, and it moaned among the pines and whistled in the crags and shouted derisive laughter as it was tossed from side to side of the rocky heights. It was like the plaint of lost souls – that is the expression Davenant made use of – the plaint of lost souls.

The road, little more than a track now, passed through this gorge, and then, after skirting a small but deep lake, which hardly knew the light of the sun, so shut in was it by overhanging trees, climbed the hill to the castle.

And the castle! Davenant used but a few words to describe it, yet somehow I could see the gloomy edifice in my mind's eye, and something of the lurking horror that it contained communicated itself to my brain. Perhaps my clairvoyant sense assisted me, for when he spoke of them I seemed already acquainted with the great stone halls, the long corridors, gloomy and cold even on the brightest and warmest of days; the dark, oak-panelled rooms, and the broad central staircase up which one of the early MacThanes had once led a dozen men on horseback in pursuit of a stag which had taken refuge within the precincts of the castle. There was the keep, too, its walls so thick that the ravages of time had made no impression upon them, and beneath the keep were dungeons which could tell terrible tales of ancient wrong and lingering pain.

Well, Mr and Mrs Davenant visited as much as the bailiff could show them of this ill-omened edifice, and Paul, for his part, thought pleasantly of his own Derbyshire home, the fine Georgian mansion, replete with every modern comfort, where he proposed to settle with his wife. And so he received something of a shock when, as they drove away, she slipped her hand into his and whispered: 'Paul, you promised, didn't you, that you would refuse me nothing?'

She had been strangely silent till she spoke these words. Paul, slightly apprehensive, assured her that she only had to ask – but the speech did not come from his heart, for he guessed vaguely what she desired.

She wanted to go and live at the castle – oh, only for a little while, for she was sure she would soon tire of it. But the bailiff had told her that there were papers, documents, which she ought to examine, since the property was now hers – and, besides, she was interested in this home of her ancestors, and wanted to explore it more thoroughly. Oh, no, she wasn't in the least influenced by the old superstition – that wasn't the attraction – she had quite got over those silly ideas. Paul had cured her, and since he himself was so convinced that they were without foundation he ought not to mind granting her her whim.

This was a plausible argument, not easy to controvert. In the end Paul yielded, though it was not without a struggle. He suggested amendments. Let him at least have the place done up for her – that would take time; or let them postpone their visit till next year – in the summer – not move in just as the winter was upon them.

But Jessica did not want to delay longer than she could help, and she hated the idea of redecoration. Why, it would spoil the illusion of the old place, and, besides, it would be a waste of money since she only wished to remain there for a week or two. The Derbyshire house was not quite ready yet; they must allow time for the paper to dry on the walls.

And so, a week later, when their stay with their friends was concluded, they went to Blackwick, the bailiff having engaged a few raw servants and generally made things as comfortable for them as possible. Paul was worried and apprehensive, but he could not admit this to his wife after having so loudly proclaimed his theories on the subject of superstition.

They had been married three months at this time – nine had passed since then, and they had never left Blackwick for more than a few hours – till now Paul had come to London – alone.

'Over and over again,' he declared, 'my wife has begged me to go. With tears in her eyes, almost upon her knees, she has entreated me to leave her, but I have steadily refused unless she will accompany me. But that is the trouble, Mr Vance, she cannot; there is something, some mysterious horror, that holds her there as surely as if she were bound with fetters. It holds her more strongly even than it held her father – we found out that he used to spend six months at least of every year at Blackwick – months when he pretended that he was travelling abroad. You see the spell – or whatever the accursed thing may be – never really relaxed its grip of him.'

'Did you never attempt to take your wife away?' asked Vance.

'Yes, several times; but it was hopeless. She would become so ill as soon as we were beyond the limit of the estate that I invariably had to take her back. Once we got as far as Dorekirk – that is the nearest town, you know – and I thought I should be successful if only I could get through the night. But she escaped me; she climbed out of a window – she meant to go back on foot, at night, all those long miles. Then I have had doctors down; but it is I who wanted the doctors, not she. They have ordered me away, but I have refused to obey them till now.'

'Is your wife changed at all – physically?' interrupted Vance.

Davenant reflected. 'Changed,' he said, 'yes, but so subtly that I hardly know how to describe it. She is more beautiful than ever – and yet it isn't the same beauty, if you can understand me. I have spoken of her white complexion, well, one is more than ever conscious of it now, because her lips have become so red – they are almost like a splash of blood upon her face. And the upper one has a peculiar curve that I don't think it had before, and when she laughs she doesn't smile – do you know what I mean? Then her hair – it has lost its wonderful gloss. Of course, I know she is fretting about me; but that is so peculiar, too, for at times, as I have told you, she will implore me to go and leave her, and then, perhaps only a few minutes later, she will wreathe her arms round my neck and say she cannot live without me. And I feel that there is a struggle going on within her, that she is only yielding slowly to the horrible influence – whatever it is – that she is herself when she begs me to go. But when she entreats me to stay – and it is then that her fascination is most intense – oh, I can't help remembering what she told me before we were married, and that word' – he lowered his voice – 'the word "vampire" – '

He passed his hand over his brow that was wet with perspiration. 'But that's absurd, ridiculous,' he muttered; 'these fantastic beliefs have been exploded years ago. We live in the twentieth century.'

A pause ensued, then Vance said quietly, 'Mr Davenant, since you have taken me into your confidence, since you have found doctors of no avail, will you let me try to help you? I think I may be of some use – if it is not already too late. Should you agree, Mr Dexter and I will accompany you, as you have suggested, to Blackwick Castle as early as possible – by tonight's mail North. Under ordinary circumstances, I should tell you, as you value your life, not to return – '

Davenant shook his head. 'That is advice which I should never take,' he declared. 'I had already decided, under any circumstances, to travel North tonight. I am glad that you both will accompany me.'

And so it was decided. We settled to meet at the station, and presently Paul Davenant took his departure. Any other details that remained to be told he would put us in possession of during the course of the journey.

'A curious and most interesting case,' remarked Vance when we were alone. 'What do you make of it, Dexter?'

'I suppose,' I replied cautiously, 'that there is such a thing as vampirism even in these days of advanced civilisation? I can understand the evil influence that a very old person may have upon a young one if they happen to be in constant intercourse – the worn-out tissue sapping healthy vitality for their own support. And there are certain people – I could think of several myself – who seem to depress one and undermine one's energies, quite unconsciously of course, but one feels somehow that vitality has passed from oneself to them. And in this case, when the force is centuries old, expressing itself, in some mysterious way, through Davenant's wife, is it not feasible to believe that he may be physically affected by it, even though the whole thing is sheerly mental?'

'You think, then,' demanded Vance, 'that it is sheerly mental? Tell me, if that is so, how do you account for the marks on Davenant's throat?'

This was a question to which I found no reply, and though I pressed him for his views, Vance would not commit himself further just then.

Of our long journey to Scotland I need say nothing. We did not reach Blackwick Castle till late in the afternoon of the following day. The place was just as I had conceived it – as I have already described it. And a sense of gloom settled upon me as our car jolted us over the rough road that led through the Gorge of the Winds – a gloom that deepened when we penetrated into the vast cold hall of the castle.

Mrs Davenant, who had been informed by telegram of our arrival, received us cordially. She knew nothing of our actual mission, regarding us merely as friends of her husband's. She was most solicitous on his behalf, but there was something strained about her tone, and it made me feel vaguely uneasy. The impression that I got was that the woman was impelled to everything that she said or did by some force outside herself – but, of course, this was a conclusion that the circumstances I was aware of might easily have conduced to. In every

other respect she was charming, and she had an extraordinary fascination of appearance and manner that made me readily understand the
force of a remark made by Davenant during our journey.

'I want to live for Jessica's sake. Get her away from Blackwick,
Vance, and I feel that all will be well. I'd go through hell to have her
restored to me – as she was.'

And now that I have seen Mrs Davenant I realised what he meant
by those last words. Her fascination was stronger than ever, but it
was not a natural fascination – not that of a normal woman, such as
she had been. It was the fascination of a Circe, of a witch, of an
enchantress – and as such was irresistible.

We had strong proof of the evil within her soon after our arrival. It
was a test that Vance had quietly prepared. Davenant had mentioned
that no flowers grew at Blackwick, and Vance declared that we
must take some with us as a present for the lady of the house. He
purchased a bouquet of pure white roses at the little town where we
left the train, for the motor-car had been sent to meet us.

Soon after our arrival he presented these to Mrs Davenant. She
took them, it seemed to me nervously, and hardly had her hand
touched them before they fell to pieces, in a shower of crumpled
petals, to the floor.

'We must act at once,' said Vance to me when we were descending
to dinner that night. 'There must be no delay.'

'What are you afraid of?' I whispered.

'Davenant has been absent a week,' he replied grimly. 'He is
stronger than when he went away, but not strong enough to survive
the loss of more blood. He must be protected. There is danger
tonight.'

'You mean from his wife?' I shuddered at the ghastliness of the
suggestion.

'That is what time will show.' Vance turned to me and added a few
words with intense earnestness. 'Mrs Davenant, Dexter, is at present
hovering between two conditions. The evil thing has not yet completely mastered her – you remember what Davenant said, how she
would beg him to go away and at the next moment entreat him to
stay? She has made a struggle, but she is gradually succumbing, and
this last week, spent here alone, has strengthened the evil. And that is
what I have got to fight, Dexter – it is to be a contest of will, a contest
that will go on silently till one or the other obtains the mastery. If
you watch you may see. Should a change show itself in Mrs Davenant
you will know that I have won.'

Thus I knew the direction in which my friend proposed to act. It was to be a war of his will against the mysterious power that had laid its curse upon the house of MacThane. Mrs Davenant must be released from the fatal charm that held her.

And I, knowing what was going on, was able to watch and understand. I realised that the silent contest had begun even while we sat at dinner. Mrs Davenant ate practically nothing and seemed ill at ease; she fidgeted in her chair, talked a great deal, and laughed – it was the laugh without a smile, as Davenant had described it. And as soon as she was able she withdrew.

Later, as we sat in the drawing-room, I could still feel the clash of wills. The air in the room felt electric and heavy, charged with tremendous but invisible forces. And outside, round the castle, the wind whistled and shrieked and moaned – it was as if all the dead and gone MacThanes, a grim army, had collected to fight the battle of their race.

And all this while we four in the drawing-room were sitting and talking the ordinary commonplaces of after-dinner conversation! That was the extraordinary part of it – Paul Davenant suspected nothing, and I, who knew, had to play my part. But I hardly took my eyes from Jessica's face. When would the change come, or was it, indeed, too late?

At last Davenant rose and remarked that he was tired and would go to bed. There was no need for Jessica to hurry. He would sleep that night in his dressing-room, and did not want to be disturbed.

And it was at that moment, as his lips met hers in a good night kiss, as she wreathed her enchantress arms about him, careless of our presence, her eyes gleaming hungrily, that the change came.

It came with a fierce and threatening shriek of wind, and a rattling of the casement, as if the horde of ghosts without was about to break in upon us. A long, quivering sigh escaped from Jessica's lips, her arms fell from her husband's shoulders, and she drew back, swaying a little from side to side.

'Paul,' she cried, and somehow the whole timbre of her voice was changed, 'what a wretch I've been to bring you back to Blackwick, ill as you are! But we'll go away, dear; yes, I'll go, too. Oh, will you take me away – take me away tomorrow?' She spoke with an intense earnestness – unconscious all the time of what had been happening to her. Long shudders were convulsing her frame. 'I don't know why I've wanted to stay here,' she kept repeating. 'I hate the place, really – it's evil – evil.'

Having heard these words I exulted, for surely Vance's success was assured. But I was soon to learn that the danger was not yet past.

Husband and wife separated, each going to their own room. I noticed the grateful, if mystified, glance that Davenant threw at Vance, vaguely aware, as he must have been, that my friend was somehow responsible for what had happened. It was settled that plans for departure were to be discussed on the morrow.

'I have succeeded,' Vance said hurriedly, when we were alone, 'but the change may be transitory. I must keep watch tonight. Go you to bed, Dexter, there is nothing that you can do.'

I obeyed – though I would sooner have kept watch, too – watch against a danger of which I had no understanding. I went to my room, a gloomy and sparsely furnished apartment, but I knew that it was quite impossible for me to think of sleeping. And so, dressed as I was, I went and sat by the open window, for now the wind that had raged round the castle had died down to a low moaning in the pine trees – a whimpering of time-worn agony.

And it was as I sat thus that I became aware of a white figure that stole out from the castle by a door I could not see, and, with hands clasped, ran swiftly across the terrace to the wood. I had but a momentary glance, but I felt convinced that the figure was that of Jessica Davenant.

And instinctively I knew that some great danger was imminent. It was, I think, the suggestion of despair conveyed by those clasped hands. At any rate, I did not hesitate. My window was some height from the ground, but the wall below was ivy-clad and afforded good foot-hold. The descent was quite easy. I achieved it, and was just in time to take up the pursuit in the right direction, which was into the thickness of the wood that clung to the slope of the hill.

I shall never forget that wild chase. There was just sufficient room to enable me to follow the rough path, which, luckily, since I had now lost sight of my quarry, was the only possible way that she could have taken; there were no intersecting tracks, and the wood was too thick on either side to permit of deviation.

And the wood seemed full of dreadful sound – moaning and wailing and hideous laughter. The wind, of course, and the screaming of night birds – once I felt the fluttering of wings in close proximity to my face. But I could not rid myself of the thought that I, in turn, was being pursued, that the forces of hell were combined against me.

The path came to an abrupt end on the border of the sombre lake that I have already mentioned. And now I realised that I was indeed only just in time, for before me, plunging knee-deep in the water, I recognised the white-clad figure of the woman I had been pursuing. Hearing my footsteps, she turned her head, and then threw up her arms and screamed. Her red hair fell in heavy masses about her shoulders, and her face, as I saw it that moment, was hardly human for the agony of remorse that it depicted.

'Go!' she screamed. 'For God's sake let me die!'

But I was by her side almost as she spoke. She struggled with me – sought vainly to tear herself from my clasp – implored me, with panting breath, to let her drown.

'It's the only way to save him!' she gasped. 'Don't you understand that I am a thing accursed? For it is I – I – who have sapped his life-blood! I know it now, the truth has been revealed to me tonight! I am a vampire, without hope in this world or the next, so for his sake – for the sake of his unborn child – let me die – let me die!'

Was ever so terrible an appeal made? Yet I – what could I do? Gently I overcame her resistance and drew her back to shore. By the time I reached it she was lying a dead weight upon my arm. I laid her down upon a mossy bank, and, kneeling by her side, gazed into her face.

And then I knew that I had done well. For the face I looked upon was not that of Jessica the vampire, as I had seen it that afternoon, it was the face of Jessica, the woman whom Paul Davenant had loved.

And later Aylmer Vance had his tale to tell.

'I waited,' he said, 'until I knew that Davenant was asleep, and then I stole into his room to watch by his bedside. And presently she came, as I guessed she would, the vampire, the accursed thing that has preyed upon the souls of her kin, making them like to herself when they too have passed into Shadowland, and gathering sustenance for her horrid task from the blood of those who are alien to her race. Paul's body and Jessica's soul – it is for one and the other, Dexter, that we have fought.'

'You mean,' I hesitated, 'Zaida, the witch!'

'Even so,' he agreed. 'Here is the evil spirit that has fallen like a blight upon the house of MacThane. But now I think she may be exorcised for ever.'

'Tell me.'

'She came to Paul Davenant last night, as she must have done before, in the guise of his wife. You know that Jessica bears a strong resemblance to her ancestress. He opened his arms, but she was foiled of her prey, for I had taken my precautions; I had placed That

upon Davenant's breast while he slept which robbed the vampire of
her power of ill. She sped wailing from the room – a shadow – she
who a minute before had looked at him with Jessica's eyes and
spoken to him with Jessica's voice. Her red lips were Jessica's lips,
and they were close to his when his eyes opened and he saw her as she
was – a hideous phantom of the corruption of the ages. And so the
spell was removed, and she fled away to the place whence she had
come – '

He paused. 'And now?' I inquired.

'Blackwick Castle must be razed to the ground,' he replied. 'That
is the only way. Every stone of it, every brick, must be ground to
powder and burnt with fire, for therein is the cause of all the evil.
Davenant has consented.'

'And Mrs Davenant?'

'I think,' Vance answered cautiously, 'that all may be well with her.
The curse will be removed with the destruction of the castle. She has
not – thanks to you – perished under its influence. She was less guilty
than she imagined – herself preyed upon rather than preying. But
can't you understand her remorse when she realised, as she was
bound to realise, the part she had played? And the knowledge of the
child to come – its fatal inheritance – '

'I understand,' I muttered with a shudder. And then, under my
breath, I whispered, 'Thank God!'

The Boy of Blackstock

HAVE INTERESTING CASE ON HAND. IF NOTHING BETTER TO DO, JOIN ME TOMORROW, HEDSTONE, ESSEX.

Such was the wording of a telegram which I received (at the little French watering-place where I happened to be staying) from Aylmer Vance, whom I imagined to be somewhere in Syria, busy with the exploration of certain ancient ruins.

It was autumn, and I, for my part, was getting tired of a rather purposeless Continental ramble, so I hailed Vance's telegram with joy. I cabled back that I was coming at once, caught a night boat from Dieppe, spent an hour or two in London, and arrived at Hedstone Grange, my friend's house in Essex, in time for lunch.

He would not say a word about the 'case', however, until we had disposed of that meal and were lazily indulging in dessert. For himself he ate very little but fruit and vegetables at any time.

'Syria will keep till later on,' he observed then. 'I had decided to go, and ran down to Hedstone to get a few things together. And then I received a visit from a certain gentleman, and – well, it promised to be interesting, so I sent you that cable.'

He interrupted my expression of pleasure that he had done so by asking a question. 'Do you know the meaning of the term "Poultergeist", Dexter?' he inquired.

I had heard the expression. 'Isn't it a German word that expresses a sort of mischievous ghost?' I replied. 'An elemental spirit that pulls furniture about, rings bells, smashes crockery, and makes itself generally obnoxious? Is that the kind of thing that we've to deal with this time?'

Aylmer smiled. 'Perhaps,' he responded with his usual caution. 'But there are circumstances about this "Poultergeist" – if the term is at all relevant – that lifts it above the common. The ghost of Blackstock Priory – where we are invited to go tomorrow – is really a family spectre, and it bears a name that is traditional – the Mischievous Boy of Blackstock – you may have heard of it, for the old legend is quite well-known. It belongs to the Rystone family. Lord Rystone owns Blackstock Priory to this day, though the possession was once very bitterly disputed.'

'I've an idea that I've heard the story,' I put in here, 'but I should like you to refresh my memory.'

'The tradition goes back to the Stuart times,' resumed Vance, 'and, of course, there is a tragedy connected with it. The Lord Rystone of that day happened to have a very beautiful young wife of whom he was immensely proud, and at the same time, inordinately jealous – probably with good reason, for she appears to have been as frivolous as she was beautiful. Anyhow, the story goes that one day he surprised his wife, under compromising conditions, in the company of a certain handsome young fellow named Gregory Laidlaw, who was the son of the very man who disputed Lord Rystone's title to the property of Blackstock. Well, the husband's jealousy and wrath got the better of him, and he murdered them both upon the spot – murdered them in cold blood just where he had found them, in a certain room at Blackstock Priory which, at that time, was his wife's boudoir. He then reported what he had done, and, in the result, was acquitted – or received no punishment worth speaking about.

'But he wasn't let off so easily by his victim, Gregory Laidlaw. Lord Rystone continued to live at Blackstock, which, by the way, is in Essex, and at no great distance from here, but his life was made a burden for him. The "Mischievous Boy" soon began his pranks. I take it that the term "Boy" has been applied to Gregory Laidlaw, or, rather, to Gregory Laidlaw's ghost, more on account of the monkey-tricks that he perpetrated than because of his actual age – according to the story, he must have been at least twenty-three or twenty-four when he was murdered. Anyway, he gave Lord Rystone no peace, never making himself actually visible, but playing most ridiculous pranks at inopportune times – throwing open doors, wailing and laughing about the corridors, pealing the bells, and often frightening people out of their wits by touching them with his cold, clammy hands.

'Well, this went on for months and months, until one day Lord Rystone did actually see his enemy. Something – heaven knows what – took him to the room where the tragedy had been enacted – he said he obeyed an impulse that he couldn't resist – and there he saw both his victims, and Gregory, his hand upon his heart and a derisive smile upon his lips, bowed to him three times. A few days later Lord Rystone died.

'After that, Master Gregory played no more pranks unless his room – the scene of his murder – was interfered with – which it was by several subsequent Lord Rystones. People who were given that room to sleep in were frightened out of their wits – their bedclothes were pulled off them or they were jerked about in the most uncomfortable fashion – but the Boy himself was not seen. He appeared only once to each Lord Rystone in succession – and that was as a foreteller of death.

'At last the Rystones became sick of their ancestral ghost, and let the Priory on a ninety-nine years' lease to the then representative of the Laidlaw family – which was really as it should be, for the Laidlaws were the first owners of the property which they had been unfairly jostled out of. They were Essex people, which the Rystones were not, and had always been popular in the country. As soon as Mr Laidlaw came into possession he had the haunted room shut up, and from that day on nothing whatever was heard of the "Mischievous Boy".'

Aylmer Vance paused and carefully peeled the skin from an apple to which he had just helped himself. Having consumed the fruit, he resumed: 'The lease granted to the Laidlaws has now expired, and the present Lord Rystone, who appears to be a man of obstinate and cantankerous temper, has refused to renew it. He has, in fact, elected to go and live at Blackstock himself.'

'And the "Mischievous Boy" has broken out again,' I hazarded, 'and is giving him a warm time of it?'

'That is so.' Aylmer smiled his slow smile. 'Lord Rystone refuses, however, to believe that there is any truth in the old tradition, and maintains that he is being made the victim of a conspiracy. He suspects some agent of his late tenant's to be at the bottom of the whole thing – for the Laidlaws want to get back to Blackstock, and the people of the neighbourhood want nothing so much as to see them reinstated. In spite of this belief, he has come to me, which proves that there is some latent superstition about him, though he won't admit it.'

'Or, of course,' I ventured, 'there may be some other natural cause for what is going on. I know that this sort of thing is usually associated with a human subject – some hysterical individual affected, perhaps, by the old tradition. Doesn't the "Poultergeist" usually act through a human medium? You have told me of such cases. There was Halton Manor, for instance. Do you know anything of Lord Rystone's family?'

Vance nodded appreciatively. He liked me to show an intelligent interest in his cases.

'I know very little further at present,' he responded. 'Lord Rystone was not very communicative. It appears that he has been in residence at Blackstock for about a month, and I imagine that there is no-one in the family except himself, his wife, his two boys, and their tutor. The boys are his sons by his first wife, for you may remember that it is only a couple of years since he married for the second time. His wife is ever so much younger than himself, and she was, I believe, the daughter of a clergyman, quite a poor man, who is now the vicar of Blackstock. These things I know from hearsay – local gossip. I've met the vicar – his name is Gaynor – the Revd Alison Gaynor – at some county function. An able man, from all accounts, and one who is ambitious for higher things. Of course, he obtained his present living through the influence of his son-in-law. But, for the moment, all this is outside the question. The point we have to solve is whether the manifestations at Blackstock are of human or superhuman origin – and we'll get to work tomorrow. I've mentioned that I propose to bring a friend with me, so you are expected.'

The next day, accordingly, we proceeded by car to Blackstock Priory, which is situated to the north-east of the county, a lonely and rather uninviting spot not far away from the sea.

We arrived in the course of the afternoon, and we found the whole household, together with one or two visitors, in the garden, partaking of tea under a huge oak that was still leafy in spite of its great age.

Lord Rystone came forward to receive us, and I was formally introduced.

The man's appearance did not impress me favourably. I could readily understand why Vance had described him as an obstinate, pigheaded man. He had a square jaw and an ugly mouth that had a way of twisting sarcastically when he spoke. One could imagine him capable of saying most unpleasant things upon the slightest provocation. He had black hair and black bushy eyebrows which came close together over the bridge of his nose. I put him down as being about fifty years of age, perhaps a little more.

His voice was loud and raucous.

'Glad to know you, Mr Dexter,' he said, 'and I hope you and Mr Vance will find means to put an end to this infernal nuisance that I've got to submit to in this house. Of course, I don't believe for a moment that it's anything to do with spooks, and the story of the Mischievous Boy is nothing but a silly superstition. No, sir, I don't believe in spooks, and I can tell you straight away that I suspect my servants. There are people about the place who have a spite against me and who want nothing better than to turn me out. They think they can frighten me away, but that's where they are mistaken. I'm not the kind of man to give in when I've made up my mind about a thing.'

It wasn't the time to argue the point, so I merely made some commonplace observation, after which I was introduced to the rest of the company.

Naturally, my interest at that moment was centred upon Lady Rystone.

She was charmingly pretty after a delicate Dresden china sort of style. She could not have been much over twenty, very fair and with tiny little hands and feet. She had eyes and lips that seemed made for love and laughter, and pretty dimples in her cheeks; but looking at her closely, one felt painfully that all these charming attributes were gradually fading, and that it would not be long before the piquante little face became pinched and fretful.

It was obvious, even to the casual observer, that she was not happy.

What on earth had induced her to marry Lord Rystone? That was the first thought that shot into my brain upon seeing her. Then I remembered that she was the daughter of a poor clergyman, and that probably family interests had been the chief factor in the case.

I felt sorry for her, for certainly she must be paying heavily for her sacrifice.

Lord Rystone's two sons, boys of twelve and fourteen years of age, were present with their tutor, whose name was James Felton. The boys were dark-haired, heavy-jowled young cubs, who had never been to school in their lives, and whose manners were atrocious.

Nor did I like the appearance of the tutor. He, too, seemed to have absorbed some of the prevailing gloom. He was a good-looking young man, but he had a discontented mouth and eyes that seemed to me shifty and untrustworthy.

The rest of the party consisted of the vicar, Lady Rystone's father, who seemed pleased to renew his acquaintance with Vance. He was a handsome man with intelligent, well-cut features; but somehow he looked no happier than the rest, and I fancied that he often glanced uneasily at his daughter. Besides him there were a couple of callers, a dull man and his even duller wife; they left soon after we arrived.

After their departure, conversation turned on the supposed haunting, and Lord Rystone repeated the story of the 'Mischievous Boy', the story with which I was already acquainted.

'There's never been a hint of a ghost at the Priory for the last hundred years,' he said. 'And looking up the records, the last allusion I can find to the "Boy's" appearance is when he appeared to my great grandfather some time in the nineteenth century, just before he died. That, of course, was years before the Priory was leased to the Laidlaws. The superstition is, you must understand, that the "Boy" only shows himself when one of our family is going to die – otherwise he is never visible; nor does he get up to his tricks unless the room in which he and his lady love were murdered is interfered with. That's the yarn they tell.'

'And you have opened up that room?' inquired Vance, who had settled himself comfortably in a deck chair.

'Yes; and why not, I should like to know?' retorted Lord Rystone with some asperity. 'It's one of the finest rooms in the house, and situated in a part of the building where it can't be easily dispensed with. It's ridiculous that it should be shut up for ever on account of an old wives' tale. I'm furnishing it as a bedroom, and eventually I shall sleep there myself.'

He spoke the last words defiantly.

'You have the courage of your opinions,' replied Vance quietly. 'But if you desire peace, might it not be just as well to try the effect of closing the room again – as an experiment?'

'No,' was the abrupt and rather surly response. 'I've told you that I don't believe there's anything supernormal in the whole business. It's all a got up job by someone who wants me to leave the place altogether. If you can prove to me the contrary, Mr Vance, then I'll shut up the room – but not until then.'

While this conversation was in progress, a conversation in which I took no part, I was watching the faces of the rest of the company, and I could not help imagining that the tutor, Mr Felton, kept his dark eyes fixed upon the face of Lady Rystone, and that she was uncomfortably aware of the fact. And I imagined that there was something malignant in his regard – almost a threat – and that he wished to convey the fact to her.

The moment, however, that he noticed that I was looking at him, he turned his attention to his pupils, to whom he made some half-laughing remark.

As for the two boys, they seemed to take the whole thing in the light of a joke, and I could see them giggling together, although they were evidently in some awe of their father.

They were ill-conditioned and badly brought up youngsters, and it naturally occurred to me that they might have something to do with the manifestations – if these really had a human origin.

Anyway, I decided to keep my eyes upon them.

'May I ask,' inquired Vance, addressing our host, 'if you opened up the haunted room as soon as you came into residence at the Priory?'

Lord Rystone shook his head.

'No,' he replied, 'it wasn't till a fortnight later.'

'And did you have any trouble during the first fortnight?'

The answer, rather grudgingly delivered, was again in the negative.

'But it was only after I'd been here a fortnight,' added his lordship, 'that the neighbourhood began to show me that I wasn't wanted. I'd taken on some of the old servants, keepers and others, who had been in the employ of my predecessors. They were a lazy lot, and I told them so – the Laidlaws have always been notorious fools in their treatment of their people – and I suppose the fellows didn't like the new administration. Anyway, they all gave notice in a body, and it was after that that the trouble began.'

'I see.'

Aylmer sat back in his chair pensively, and for a little while after that took no part in the general conversation.

One of the boys – the eldest – was recounting how he had been told that morning that one of the servants, happening to pass the door of the haunted room rather late the night before, had heard curious sounds from within, and being braver than most of his fellows, had ventured very gingerly to open the door.

It was not quite dark within, because the moon was shining, and the room, as yet only half-furnished, had not been provided with curtains, and the man declared that he caught sight of what he imagined to be two dim figures standing in the moonlight apparently clasped in each other's arms.

He was not, however, able to swear positively to anything, because before he had had time to open the door wide, it was torn from his hand and then slammed violently in his face.

Lord Rystone frowned heavily. Incredulous though he professed to be, he was palpably worried at this suggestion of the actual appearance of the 'Boy' – an appearance reputed to bode him ill.

'Who told you this absurd story, Paul?' he asked gruffly.

'It was Lomax, the under-footman,' responded the boy readily.

'Very well, go and tell Lomax that I want to speak to him at once. We may as well question him here in your presence, Mr Vance.'

Lord Rystone addressed the last words to my friend, who quietly nodded his acquiescence.

And so Paul ran off, evidently delighted with his mission, and a few minutes later returned with the under-footman who, in our presence, confirmed in every respect the story which we had just heard, adding one or two details of his own.

He had imagined that he heard voices in the room, low whisperings, and it was that which had at first attracted his attention, knowing, as he did, that the room was not yet in use, and that, in any case, nobody was likely to be there at that hour of the night.

He told his story gravely, palpably convinced of the truth of every word he said. He seemed to me a well-spoken, dependable sort of young man, and I felt genuinely sorry for him when Lord Rystone, unable to shake his story in any particular, lost his temper, addressed him roughly, and told him that he was a coward and a fool.

'Why on earth didn't you open the door again after it had been slammed in your face?' shouted the angry earl. 'I suppose you were too frightened to do so, eh?'

'I did try,' responded the young man, flushing to his hair, 'but it was no use. The door was locked.'

'Well, that's a proof that you are telling a lie,' was the fierce retort, 'for there's been no key fitted to the lock yet.' He turned to Vance and myself. 'The room had been walled up,' he explained, 'and after I had it opened up, we found an unlocked door without a key; and as I haven't got a new one yet, how was it possible that the door could be locked? The fellow's a palpable liar.'

The natural consequence of this repeated assertion was that the footman gave notice upon the spot – and I may say that I thoroughly sympathised with him under the circumstances.

Lord Rystone fumed with rage. He swore violently without the smallest regard to the presence of his wife and children.

'It's a conspiracy,' he declared, 'and they are all in it; but I'll get even with them yet.'

Soon after this we went into the house, and Vance and I were left to ourselves till dinner time.

During this interview I took the opportunity of mentioning to him the curious expression which I had seen upon the tutor's face and the significant glance which he had cast at Lady Rystone.

'I don't like the look of that fellow,' I said, 'but, of course, it may only have been my imagination. Have you formed any opinion so far?'

'It's much too early yet to form any opinion,' was my friend's reply. He smiled a little. 'You ought to know by now, Dexter,' he said, 'that I never jump to conclusions.'

At dinner that evening we were introduced to yet another member of the household – Mrs Mellish, who acted as companion to the young countess. She was an elderly and austere woman who did not in the least add to the gaiety of the company.

And it was while we were at dinner that we were treated to our first manifestation of the mischievous influence that was at work in the house.

There came a tremendous crash all of a sudden in the hall without, and on running to the door we discovered the butler standing in the midst of a debris of broken plates and dishes and other paraphernalia that he had been carrying to the dining-room upon a tray.

He was white and trembling, and he had cut his hand a little.

Lord Ryston's cheeks grew florid with rage, and he began to bluster. He had never known such gross carelessness in his life, he declared. What on earth had the man done to drop the tray?

The butler stooped and picked up something from the floor, where it lay among the fragments of broken china.

'That's what did it, your lordship,' he said nervously, holding up for our inspection a heavy flint stone. 'It fell down from overhead right into the middle of my tray. I couldn't help dropping the things, no-one could have.'

The hall was large and square, and a gallery ran round three sides of it. It would have been quite easy, I reflected, for anyone concealed up there to drop the stone as the butler passed below. But the incident made one thing practically certain: if anyone of the house party was responsible for the trouble, there must undoubtedly be a confederate as well.

For we had all, including the two boys, been assembled at the dinner table.

The boys rushed off upstairs, and for the next few minutes, while their father blustered, we could hear them careering up and down the gallery and opening every available door in their pursuit of the ghost. But their efforts were quite futile, and presently they returned, excited and looking upon the whole thing as excellent sport.

I was soon to find out that they behaved in exactly the same way after every manifestation of which they were witness.

The butler was still quaking, partly with fear and partly with wrath at the way his explanation had been received.

'I can't stand it any longer,' he muttered, stanching the blood from a small cut upon his hand. He looked almost as if he were about to faint. 'I'm sorry, my lord, but I should like to leave – tomorrow, if you will allow me.'

'Yes, go, and the devil take you,' roared his lordship furiously, after which we all returned to the dining-room and continued our interrupted meal as best we could.

Nothing further occurred till about an hour later, when we were assembled in the drawing-room, except the two boys, who had been sent off to bed.

The first intimation we had of the return of the poltergeist – if poltergeist it was – was the sudden opening of the drawing-room door. It was flung violently back, so violently as nearly to throw it off its hinges, and at the same moment I distinctly heard the sound of a chuckling laugh.

Yet, once again, when we rushed out into the hall, it was to find no trace of any living soul.

Almost immediately afterwards, however, and while we were still standing there literally gaping at each other, a series of bells began to ring, apparently from somewhere in the servants' quarters.

Poor Lady Rystone was nearly in tears – to all appearance terribly afraid.

'Oh, Kelsey,' she entreated her husband, 'what's the use of going on like this? Why won't you shut up the haunted room again, or, better still, why won't you leave this horrid place altogether?'

'I dare say you'd like me to take you away, wouldn't you?' he retorted in a tone that to me sounded quite unnecessarily brutal. 'But I've had enough of London, and so have you, for some time to come. And as for shutting up the haunted room, I am damned if I do. I'll get to the bottom of this infernal conspiracy first.'

There was something terrifying in the frown he bestowed upon his wife, and Lady Rystone seemed to shrink under it – her lips quivered pitifully, and she shook in every limb. I felt more sorry for her than ever, and deeply incensed against the man for his sheer brutality. I was puzzled, too, for at the same moment I was again conscious of that queer, menacing look in the tutor's eyes as he watched the scene. There was something horribly exultant about it – I think that is the word that most nearly expresses my meaning.

Well, we had no more alarms that night, and the next day Vance and I set about making a thorough exploration of the Priory, which,

I don't think I have mentioned, was a low-built, rambling edifice with walls of considerable thickness.

I suspected secret chambers and passages, and, indeed, several of these were known and pointed out to us by Lord Rystone. For the most part, however, they had been blocked up so efficiently as to render them impossible as hiding-places.

We examined the haunted room.

It was a large, low apartment upon the first floor. After its use as a boudoir by the murdered Lady Rystone, it had been used as a bedroom, and then dismantled because of the hauntings. It was at present unfurnished save for a few old-fashioned chairs and a sofa. It had a painted ceiling, and its walls were hung with faded tapestry. There were one or two curtained recesses which added to the eerie aspect of the room.

'With your permission, Lord Rystone,' said Vane, 'I will pass the night in this room. You need not worry about the bed. I shall be quite comfortable in one of the chairs.'

Permission was granted, and then, very naturally, I asked Vance to allow me to share his vigil. But to my surprise, and a little to my mortification, he refused.

He laid his hand in a friendly manner upon my shoulder.

'Don't be vexed, Dexter,' he said. 'I have my reasons. Believe me, it is for the best.'

He would not give his reasons, and I knew him well enough by now to appreciate that argument was useless, so I was forced to accept the inevitable.

Well, I had thought out all manner of plans for trapping the 'ghost', if the 'ghost' should prove to be human – thread entanglements over the bell-wires, and that sort of thing – but Vance would have none of them.

'Wait till tomorrow,' he said. 'I shall know better then how to act.'

I could not induce him to tell me his suspicions, yet I knew they were already forming in his mind.

At dinner that night there was another unpleasant scene – not due this time to ghostly phenomena.

Lord Rystone came in palpably in a bad temper. He attacked his wife almost before a particle of food had passed his lips.

'Your father's been to see me privately this afternoon, Elsa. Do you know why?'

It was his tone rather than what he said that implied wrath.

She looked up – eagerly, I thought.

'No, Kelsey; what was it?'

'He's giving up his living – the living he begged me for and which I gave him. He's quite independent of me now, if you please. They want him in a large London parish, and I suppose we shall hear of him being made a bishop next. And not a word of gratitude. A wretched, penniless curate whom I set on his feet because I happened to take a fancy to his daughter! He fawned about my neck as long as there was anything to be got out of me, but now I may go hang.'

He muttered other things which were only half audible, luckily.

I watched Lady Rystone and wondered at the joy which I read in her eyes – joy which her disconcerted air at this public outbreak could not quite conceal.

She made no retort, carefully avoiding to say a word which might still further incense her husband, and as soon as possible turned the conversation into a safer channel. But I think that Vance, like myself, noticed her flushed cheeks and eager expression.

We had very little in the way of phenomena that evening, and at ten o'clock we parted for the night. Vance went to the haunted room, and I saw him no more till the morning.

He came to me quite early – before I was up – and sat on the edge of my bed.

'Dexter,' he said gravely, 'we have got to give up this job; it isn't in our line. I wish we could leave today, but there are people asked to meet us at dinner. However, tomorrow – '

I sat up in bed in my surprise.

'Vance,' I exclaimed, 'have you solved the mystery?'

He inclined his head. His face was more than usually serious.

'Yes,' he said.

'Won't you tell me?'

'When we get home – not now. There's still some work that I must do – and it is no pleasant task. But this I want to ask you – don't trouble me with questions till we are clear of Blackstock Priory.'

I promised that I would not; but, needless to say, I was puzzled to a degree. However, as fate would have it, the day did not pass without my making a discovery on my own account.

It happened in the course of the afternoon.

Vance had gone out on some errand with which he had not acquainted me, and I was amusing myself with a book in the garden. It was a hot day, and I had found a comfortable nook, screened by trees, close to a little glade, where there was a marble seat – probably a trophy carried off from some ancient Italian palace.

I must have dropped off to sleep, for I can only remember starting up at the sound of voices in the glade – from which I was completely hidden.

A woman was speaking – I recognised the voice of Lady Rystone.

'You are an unutterable blackguard' – that is what I heard her say – 'a loathsome blackmailer! But you daren't do what you threaten.'

'Why not?'

The answer came in the suave, unpleasing voice of Felton, the tutor.

'Because, however much you might hurt me, my husband would thrash you as you deserve.'

'That may be.' The man gave an ugly laugh. 'Nevertheless, my lady, I refuse to abate one jot of my demand. A thousand pounds – and I know that you've got the money – that you've been saving up for contingencies – pawning your jewels. You could give me that sum without hurting yourself. Come, be sensible.' His voice had a persuasive note in it now. 'I don't want to hurt you, but I'm hard up – desperate. Like yourself, I want to get away from this accursed place and from those two unlicked cubs I'm supposed to look after. And I can only do it by putting pressure upon you – now that I've found you out. Think of the scandal, my lady, if it became known that the "Mischievous Boy of Blackstock"' – he laughed again – 'is no other than your lover, in order to avoid whom your husband took you away from London, because he had begun to have his suspicions? Supposing Lord Rystone knew – as I know – that this man can get in and out of the Priory as he pleases by means of a secret passage opening into the so-called haunted room? That as long as the haunted room was shut off, you were both quite happy, since you, my lady, had secret access to it as well; but when it was opened up, your trysting place was no longer safe, so you had to have recourse to the old superstition in order to frighten his lordship into walling it off again – or, better still, to compel him to leave the Priory altogether. Supposing all this were known, what then?'

My horror at hearing this cold-blooded revelation may be imagined. I hated to think that, all unwittingly, I had been an eavesdropper; but from the first it was impossible for me to reveal myself – it might only have made matters worse – and I could not steal away without betraying my presence.

So this was the pitiful explanation of the mystery – this was what Vance, too, had found out and refused to tell me!

I could understand his reluctance now!

It was all I could do to restrain myself from springing out of my hiding-place and laying violent hands upon the vile blackmailer – every nerve in my body tingled with the desire to pay him in different coin to what he demanded – but I kept myself in control.

And of the rest of that abominable interview I need record no more than this: Felton accorded his victim a period of twenty-four hours in which to make up her mind. Unless he received his pound of flesh upon the following day, he would unfailingly betray Lady Rystone to her husband.

I waited impatiently for Vance's return, and when, late that afternoon, we met, I told him everything.

He was deeply concerned, for of this trouble threatening Lady Rystone he was quite unaware.

'Twenty-four hours' grace,' he muttered. 'This is serious, Dexter, very serious. For I can foresee what will happen. Lady Rystone and her lover – for it's true about the lover, unfortunately true – will act at once – tonight, instead of waiting till tomorrow, as they proposed.'

He wrinkled up his brows in deep thought. I did not understand what he meant, so after a few minutes he proceeded to enlighten me.

He told me of his experiences the night before.

'I had my suspicions,' he said. 'You see, I had had a chat with Gaynor in the garden the day we arrived. The vicar confided to me that his daughter was unhappy – that she was being treated like a prisoner – always watched except when she was in the house – that unpleasant woman, Mrs Mellish, you know. She was too fond of gaiety, and there was a man who was fond of her – a man named Frank Prescot. Anyway, Lord Rystone became jealous and carried her off to Blackstock. And Mr Gaynor blamed himself bitterly. You see, it was on his account that his daughter married – in order that he might get the living and the benefits.

'Well, these things made me suspicious – and I formed my own conclusions, too, by studying Lady Rystone's face. I arranged to spend a night in the haunted room. I found a secret passage – as I had expected to. It leads to a ruined chapel just outside the big wall, and it communicates with another room in the house – an empty one – as well as with the haunted room. So, you see, while the latter was shut up, two people could meet there practically with impunity. It was less safe afterwards, as we know from the experience of Lomax, the under-footman. It is evident, in that case, that the lovers had secured the key, and were able to save themselves by using it.

'And later that night I saw them. Yes, Dexter, the lovers met and never dreamed that they were watched from behind one of those curtained recesses. No-one knew that I was spending a night in the haunted room, so they had no suspicions.

'They were only together a few minutes, and it was to plan an elopement – not for tonight, because there were preparations to be made, but for tomorrow. Lady Rystone considered herself free at last. She had borne all the indignities that her husband heaped upon her because her father has been dependent upon Lord Rystone, but now – you noticed her hardly-concealed joy at dinner when she heard that Gaynor had secured his independence? – she was free to do as she liked, so she declared, and her husband had long ago forfeited, by his brutality, all right to her love. It appears he had struck her over and over again.

'And so everything was settled between them. Tomorrow night they would fly together and brave the world. But now, Dexter, I foresee that they will change their plans – that they will go to-night.'

I admitted the force of this reasoning.

'What is to be done?' I asked.

'I saw Gaynor this afternoon,' resumed Vance, 'and told him everything. His sympathies are wholly with his daughter, but he naturally wishes to save her from taking a false step. We had arranged that he should come tomorrow morning and take her away. Rystone cannot keep her in the Priory by force. And now – well, there is nothing for it but for me to return to the vicarage and warn Gaynor of what has happened. He must act at once, dinner-party or no dinner-party. He must come to the Priory this very evening, see Lady Rystone, and persuade her to go away with him. That is the only practical course.'

And this was the plan upon which we decided. Vance set off at once, and he did not return till near the dinner hour. But he had failed in his mission, for the vicar was away from home, and all efforts to find him had proved unavailing.

That hateful dinner-party – how well I remember it! The whole company seemed to be on tenterhooks, and when about ten o'clock Lady Rystone pleaded a bad headache, Vance and I glanced meaningly but helplessly at each other.

Luckily, the guests departed soon after that, and we men – with the exception of the tutor, who had pleaded some excuse – retired to Lord Rystone's study to smoke.

Half an hour later there came a horrible interruption. The door flung open, and Felton, excited and dishevelled, rushed in.

'I've come to warn you, my lord,' he cried. He gazed at us defiantly. 'I consider it my duty to do so. Your wife has introduced her lover into your house. It is he who is the author of the disturbances – which have only been contrived in order that they may continue a guilty intrigue without interruption. They are now – '

I was boiling over with rage.

'This man is a vile blackmailer,' I began, but Lord Rystone silenced me with a gesture. He had risen, and his face was congested with suppressed rage.

'Go on, Felton,' he said hoarsely. 'Where are they now?'

'In the haunted room – if you hurry you will find them there together. They are eloping – tonight.' He gnashed his teeth with the wrath of a blackmailer foiled.

Lord Rystone did not speak another word. He jerked open a door of his desk, extracted something which he held under his hand, and then, without a glance at any of us, made for the door.

He was across the hall and mounting the stairs before we had time to realise the full horror of the situation.

'Quick – he's got a revolver!' cried Vance.

He set off in pursuit, followed by myself and then by the tutor, who had turned deathly white and staggered as he went.

But Lord Rystone was fleeter than any of us. He had thrown open the door of the haunted room before any of us could come up with him. I heard him mutter a hoarse cry – then he lifted his hand and fired – the shot echoed horribly down the corridor.

The next moment Lord Rystone repeated his cry – but this time it was a scream of fear. He fired again wildly, and then, throwing up his arms, staggered back. Vance caught him as he fell.

And I – for a brief moment I was able to see through the open door into the haunted room. And I was dimly conscious of a figure – that of a young man clad in garments of a bygone day, who stood smiling and bowing towards Lord Rystone, his hand upon his heart.

The 'Mischievous Boy of Blackstock' had fulfilled his destiny.

Lord Rystone died a few days later – of a stroke of apoplexy, so the doctors declared.

And it was not many weeks later that Lady Rystone was quietly married.

The Indissoluble Bond

I have probably already made clear in these records that it was to the elucidation of certain abstruse and little known branches of psychology that my friend, Aylmer Vance, mainly directed his activities. The incidents which I will now narrate illustrate the limitation of human power – even such as his – in the face of forces which as yet we hardly realise – which are, in fact, barely conceivable to our finite intelligence.

In the course of the summer we had met in London a charming family named Verriker – Colonel Verriker, his wife, son, and daughter. It is with the latter that my story has mainly to do.

She was a charming girl, twenty-two or three years of age, and she had soft dreamy eyes, which hinted at a spirituality in contradiction to more superficial appearances. For she seemed in every sense of the word a thoroughly normal girl.

She was keen on active exercise, and did not care much for books. She was an excellent horsewoman, and rode every morning in the Row, getting up early for that purpose. She excelled at tennis and golf, and could even handle a gun – or so I was assured – without losing anything of her natural femininity. I mention these things to show that she was about the last person in the world whom one would expect to find developing attributes out of the ordinary run.

For the rest, she had a slim and lithe figure, was above the medium height, and had fine masses of chestnut hair. She was of a type that most men would admire, because of her splendid vitality and undisguised joy of life.

We struck up rather a friendship with the Verrikers that summer, and were sorry that they had to leave London before the season was actually over, returning to their own residence, which was at Sandminster – I will call it so, as it is very necessary in this case that no true names should be revealed.

The colonel was an important personage in the parochial affairs of the little cathedral town, and he could never be away for very long at a time. Before parting, however, he exacted a promise from us that we should come to stay with him later in the year.

One day Vance showed me a letter which he had received from Colonel Verriker. It contained an invitation to both of us to run down to Sandminster as soon as ever we could spare the time.

'It is not only the pleasure of your company that we desire,' so the colonel wrote, 'though that, of course, is the first consideration. The fact is, my wife and I are a little troubled about our daughter Beryl, and there are certain features in the case which make me think that you, better than most men – having regard to your deep knowledge of matters psychical – may be able to advise us. For my part, I must candidly admit that I am old-fashioned, and know practically nothing about these things. Girls get delusions into their heads at times, and, as a rule, they mean very little – but it's queer in the case of Beryl, who isn't in the least of an hysterical type. However, you shall judge for yourself, and the sooner we see you, the happier we shall be.'

As it happened, we were very busy just then – an important investigation that we could not possibly abandon – and so it was not till a full fortnight later that we were able to accept Colonel Verriker's invitation.

We reached Sandminster one afternoon early in the week. It is a charming old-world town, and the cathedral – not a large one – is famed for its beauty of architecture and for its picturesque surroundings. It stands in an open space, reached by narrow roads between high walls from the town side, while on the other there is open country. The Verrikers owned a large modern house within five minutes' walk of the cathedral.

We were most cordially received by Colonel and Mrs Verriker and by Beryl, who looked to me quite unchanged and in the best of health. Her brother was away, we were told, staying with some friends in Scotland.

It was not till the ladies had retired, after we had spent a pleasant evening together, that the colonel referred to the subject of his letter. He began by repeating what he had already said – that, for his own part, he did not think there was anything to worry about – it was his wife who was nervous.

'I fancy that my opinion was wholly justified,' he remarked. 'And I feel almost guilty for having troubled you at all. For since I wrote to you – and that's more than a fortnight ago – Beryl has been quite herself, she hasn't had a single attack. Yes, I really feel as if I owe you an apology.'

He spoke as if he were half ashamed of troubling us with the story at all.

'Miss Beryl seems to me to be in excellent health and spirits,' commented Vance, 'so let us hope that your surmise is correct. However, if you would like to confide in us – '

He spoke encouragingly; it was very evident that the colonel wished to unburden his soul.

'Well, it's like this,' was the answer. 'There were times when an extraordinary change seemed to come over Beryl's appearance and demeanour. It usually happened quite suddenly and unexpectedly, generally in the late afternoon, but I've seen it at all manner of times. One could imagine that she was listening for something, listening intently, and there was a tense, half-frightened look upon her face which, I assure you, was quite alarming. And then after a few minutes she would make some excuse, usually of a headache, and go off to her own room. If she happened to be anywhere outside at the time she would go straight home. After about an hour she would usually show up again – looking terribly pale, but in other respects quite herself. Of course, her mother and I questioned her, and we have had the doctor to see her, but he finds nothing amiss, and I expect he's right; but that curious listening attitude worried us, and then there was something else – '

He paused.

'Yes?' prompted Vance, who was listening with sympathetic interest, sitting in his favourite attitude, his elbows on his knees, his chin resting in his hands.

'Well,' continued the colonel, 'after the thing had happened several times, my wife went to see Beryl in her room, bringing her something to relieve her headache. The door was locked, and when she knocked no-one answered. Beryl's room, I must tell you, has a flight of steps leading down to the garden. Not being able to get in by the door, Mrs Verriker went round by the window. Well, the girl wasn't there, and she hadn't been lying down upon the bed – she had gone straight out again – '

'Did you ask her where she went?'

'Yes. And she had an answer ready. The air did her headache good. That may, of course, be true, but it's curious, for why did she wish to deceive us? And I'm sure it's always been the case, that she goes somewhere, and does not want to admit to us where she goes.'

'You haven't tried to follow her?'

The colonel shook his head.

'No. You see, we only arrived at a definite conclusion on the subject just before I wrote to you, and nothing has happened since. I'm hoping nothing more will happen. And I shouldn't have troubled you at all, but we were really getting alarmed. You can't imagine how strange she looks when the attack – I suppose I must call it an attack – gets hold of her.'

'At those moments,' queried Vance, 'does she seem to be acting of her own volition? Do you think she is aware of what she does?'

Colonel Verriker pondered.

'She doesn't seem to lose the sense of her own individuality,' he answered. 'But at the same time she seems to be responding to some force outside herself – if I may put it so.'

'And you say that your daughter gives you no explanation of all this, no explanation at all?'

Our host shook his head.

'She makes light of it to us,' he replied. 'Says that there is nothing the matter except for her headaches. However, as I've told you, she's been quite free from these attacks for the last fortnight, so let's hope there's nothing in it after all.'

I could see from Vance's expression that he did not hold this view. Also he continued to put questions.

'Tell me, colonel,' he said, 'have you any sort of suspicion in your own mind? Don't be afraid of telling me, however slight the point may actually seem to you. Is there, for instance, any love affair?'

'Nothing that could cause her any trouble of this sort,' responded the colonel. 'And that's a very puzzling feature of the case. Beryl has been engaged for the last four months – it happened while we were in London – to an altogether desirable young man, a Mr Geoffrey Beynion, who had just passed very creditably into the Foreign Office, and who is destined for the Indian Civil. They have decided to get married this winter. Geoffrey's at St Petersburg at present, because he's making a special study of Russian.'

'And you are sure your daughter is as fond of her fiancé as ever? For if she repented of her engagement – '

'No, I am certain it isn't that,' was the response, 'for I've questioned her very seriously on the subject. She assures me that she loves Geoffrey devotedly, and would like to hasten on the marriage if she were not afraid of interfering with his studies. In fact, it seemed to me that it was in her marriage that she looked for safety.'

'And have you noticed anything else?'

'Well' – there was a certain hesitation in the colonel's speech – 'it hardly seems worth mentioning, and yet perhaps I had better do so. Beryl has always been fond of music, and she used to love nothing better than to play the organ in the Minster whenever she got the chance. After our return from London we found that they'd got a new organist, and we attended a recital which he gave one evening. The man's playing seemed to impress my girl tremendously, and eventually she got him to give her a few lessons. It was soon after this that the trouble began, and somehow – I hardly know why – I always associate that curious listening attitude of hers with her attraction for the organ. It was just such an attitude that I noticed on the evening when we attended the recital.'

Colonel Verriker paused.

'And this man, the organist – ' prompted Vance.

'It's ridiculous, perfectly ridiculous – unthinkable – to imagine him as any sort of factor in the case,' asserted Verriker with decision. 'He's an impossible creature, the merest shadow of a man. Oh, no, he's out of the question; he's absolutely out of the question.'

Vance did not argue the point, and as there was nothing more that Colonel Verriker could tell us, it was eventually agreed that we should just wait and watch, while hoping that his surmise was correct, and that the trouble, whatever it might be, was really at an end.

And at first it seemed as if this was going to be the case, for two or three days passed pleasantly without any manifestation of unrest upon the part of Beryl.

We watched her closely, and she gave us every opportunity of doing so, for she was constantly in our company, acting as a charming cicerone in showing us the various sights of the neighbourhood. We spent a certain amount of time in the Minster, too, for there were some beautiful old brasses there of great archaeological interest, in the study of which Vance was deeply interested.

On the day of our visit to the Minster, Vance questioned Miss Verriker, in an apparently unconcerned manner, on the subject of the organ. I watched her keenly as she made answer, and her embarrassment, although she tried to hide it, was obvious. She told us that the organist, Mr Cuthbert Ford, had been laid up for the last fortnight, and that he was the most wonderful player that they had ever had at Sandminster.

As we left the church Vance whispered to me: 'The organist has been ill a fortnight – and it is a fortnight since Miss Verriker has had an attack. Do you draw any deduction, Dexter?'

His tone was ominous.

It was on the fourth day after our arrival that something happened. Several young people had been asked in the afternoon to tennis and croquet, and Beryl apparently enjoyed herself as much as anybody.

It must have been after six o'clock, and many of the guests had departed, while the few that remained were resting in basket chairs on the lawn, chatting pleasantly together.

I was quite close to Beryl, and was probably the first to notice the change come over her.

For some minutes she was very silent, sitting back in her chair. It was her racquet falling off her knees that attracted my attention to her; I noticed then that she was sitting up, that her cheeks had become pale, and that there was a look of intense eagerness upon her face.

Her eyes shone brightly, her lips were a little parted, and her fingers, lying in her lap, kept up a persistent tattoo. There was a marked straining forward of the neck, and an unmistakable suggestion in her whole attitude of listening – listening for something that was audible to her ears alone.

I spoke to her, but, for the moment, she took no notice of me, and I seized the opportunity of beckoning to Vance, who, luckily, was not far away.

He came at once, and it was just as he approached that Miss Verriker rose to her feet, without any alteration of the strained and listening attitude, and, turning to me, remarked in a tone of voice that was natural enough to deceive me if I had not been prepared for it: 'I'm sorry, Mr Dexter, but I've got a violent headache just come on. It's the sun, I expect, and I've really been rather energetic this afternoon. I must go and lie down a bit, and then I shall be all right again. You'll excuse me, I know. I'm not going to say a word to anybody, as I don't want to worry them.'

Her father and mother were engaged just then with some guests in another part of the grounds, and were therefore unaware of what was happening.

The girl hardly waited for my reply, but moved away, and Vance and I watched her disappearing in the direction of the house.

When she was out of sight Vance laid his hand upon my arm.

'Come, Dexter,' he said, 'there's work for us to do – for you especially.'

With which he led me away and into the house where, presumably, Miss Verriker had already gone.

'You wish to follow her?' I whispered. 'If so, we'd better wait somewhere outside. She goes to her room first, at least so the colonel says, locks the door so that people should think she's still there, and then makes her way out by the window.'

'No, we are not going to follow her – at any rate, not in the flesh; but you shall do so, Dexter, in the spirit.'

I knew what he meant. He was going to make use of my clairvoyant power.

I nodded without further remark, and together we went to my room, where I allowed him to put me to sleep as he had done on many other occasions.

In my hand I held a glove belonging to Miss Verriker, which she had dropped in her hasty departure, and which Vance had picked up and brought to the house with him.

Well, it was not long before my vision began to develop itself, a vision more vivid than any I have ever experienced. I will try to relate exactly what I saw and what I heard – for in these trances I am as keenly susceptible to sound as to sight.

That the exact words which I record were actually spoken I cannot assert – but I had the impression of them, most definite and unmistakable.

I found myself gazing into a narrow, dark room, so dark that it was some time before I realised from the array of tall painted pipes that it was the organ loft of the Minster.

But by degrees I began to see more clearly. The last long beams of the sun, now near its setting, shimmered through the diamond-shaped pane and rested upon a pair of hands which were dreamily hovering over the keyboard.

So thin and white were these hands that I almost imagined them transparent, perforated by the rays, and I remember that it seemed to me for a moment that it must be a spirit and not a man who was seated there at the organ.

Yet this was not so, for the face, as soon as I could discern it more clearly, was palpably of human flesh and blood. But how thin and sunken! The cheekbones stood out in painful prominence, and the eyes glittered from deep sockets cruelly black-rimmed. So this must be Cuthbert Ford, the man of whom Colonel Verriker had spoken to us.

He was sitting there playing the organ, making strange and weird music, the sound of which reached my ears distinctly, though it was all of the substance of a dream.

It was the strangest music that I have ever listened to, unlike that of any composer, living or dead, and I knew instinctively that the player must love the instrument he played upon so passionately as to give his very soul to it.

I felt that he himself, sitting alone in the narrow loft with the twilight creeping about him, with the great church holy in its emptiness, had become bereft of feeling, devoid of emotion, while the organ, to him, was a sentient being.

The man had developed his spirit at the expense of his body, and his spirit sang in harmony with the music of the organ – merged in it – was it.

I listened, overwhelmed with emotion such as I had never felt before. The organ breathed softly of dead hopes and strange desires – the unknown and unknowable.

To have understood would have meant the solution of the mystery of the soul of man – and I knew that it was best not to understand.

Suddenly there came a step upon the narrow wooden staircase that led to the organ loft. The sound appeared to disturb the player, and instantly the tone of his music changed.

The church resounded with the conventional strains of Beethoven.

The door opened, and Beryl Verriker entered. She was clad in the light afternoon frock which she had been wearing for the tennis party. She was intensely pale.

She stood a while silent by his side while he continued to play the familiar sonata. Then she touched his arm.

'Why do you play that now?' she said. 'It is Beethoven, not you.'

He stopped and turned to her.

'Well?' he inquired.

'You called me, Cuthbert,' she murmured. Her voice trembled, and I knew that she was shuddering from head to foot.

'You heard me?' he said. His voice sounded hoarse and unsympathetic, as ugly and as unpleasing as the man's whole personality.

'You heard me,' he repeated, 'and you were bound to obey. When soul speaks to soul, Beryl, the flesh is powerless to resist.'

'I know it too well.' Her voice was full of shuddering awe. She seated herself on the bench beside him. 'You are murdering my body, and it's wicked, it's cruel.' She buried her face in her hands. 'For I want to live, I want to live!'

He made no answer for a few moments, but his eyes, those eyes in which all the life of him seemed to be concentrated, blazed upon her out of their hollow sockets.

'How do I hurt you?' he said at last, and there was a deep irony in his tone. 'I've spoken no word to you of love, and I know, as well as you know yourself, that every nerve of your body revolts from me. But over your soul, Beryl, I have a right, since I have the power to command it. And if, through the harmony of the organ, I can speak to you of the beauty of the soul, freed from the hampering prison of its vile earthly body, of spiritual love undreamed of in this hollow world, of things beyond the comprehension of human sense, then I am doing what your soul must be grateful for – I am fulfilling destiny – but leading you to the achievement of the inevitable.'

He caught her hands in his, those gaunt bony hands, and I saw her tremble at his touch.

'Our souls belong to each other, Beryl,' he said. 'They have belonged to each other through the long dark ages of the past, they will be in harmony through the infinite aeons of futurity. You are mine – shall I prove it to you?'

As he spoke his hands left hers and once more began to press the notes of the organ. Again that strange, weird harmony sprang into being – a call of spirit to spirit – and I could see that Beryl's eyes were closing dreamingly; then suddenly, with a violent struggle, she seemed to recover herself. In her turn she seized the man's hands and dragged them from the keyboard.

Then, panting, she closed the lid.

'Stop playing that music! Stop, I say!' she cried passionately. 'Things must not go on as they are. You have bewitched me. I don't understand myself. But it must cease. I say it must cease!'

He looked at her, and all the vitality of his poor body leaped to his eyes.

'You have given me your soul, Beryl,' he said. 'You would not take it away – now? But you cannot – it is beyond your power.'

'I have not given it,' she panted. 'You have tried to steal it from me, thief that you are! But, still, my soul is my own!'

'So speaks the body,' he replied, with a shrug of his humped shoulders. 'What does it know of the desires of the soul?'

'I hate you with my body and with my soul!' she gasped. 'I loathe and abhor you.'

'You are wrong,' he replied callously; 'and I've only to touch the organ' – he seemed about to raise the lid.

'No,' she murmured despairingly. 'Spare me, Cuthbert, I'm not strong enough to resist you. I know it. But I'm going to plead with you for mercy. Listen! I am young, and the world is very sweet to me. I want to live, to enjoy my life. It is only a few short years, after all, in comparison with the eternity of which you have spoken. I want warm, human love, Cuthbert, and I know nothing – understand, nothing – of the love of the spirit. I have never told you, have I, that I'm engaged to be married, and that I love the man who will be my husband? I want to give myself to him body and soul – '

'You cannot give the latter,' he interrupted grimly.

'I can, if you will let me,' she pleaded. 'Release me from this bondage; it is bad for us both – unnatural, wicked. It will kill me.'

'And is not that a consummation to be desired?' he cried fiercely. 'To pass from this hateful existence of pain and misery and vain hopes to the freedom of spiritual happiness?'

'I do not want to die. I love, and love is life.'

'Sordid lusts of the flesh!' he retorted contemptuously. 'I tell you that your spirit is mine, and shall be mine through all eternity. It is fate, and you cannot struggle against it.'

He paused, and for a few moments there was silence in the organ loft. I could hear the girl's quiet sobbing and the hard breathing of the man as he sat huddled up by her side.

At last he spoke, and again the tone of biting irony was evident in his words.

'What matter a year or two, when we have eternity before us? It shall be as you desire. You ask for freedom in this life. You crave for the gratification of the flesh. Go, then – while I live I shall call upon my fellow soul no more.'

She sprang to her feet with joy.

'You promise me this – oh! you do promise it?' she cried. 'Thank God! Thank God! Then I am free!'

'Remember,' he continued, with unaltered expression, 'I said, "while I live". Look at me.'

She looked, and then sank down upon the bench with a shuddering cry. For she read death in every line of his face.

For a short space neither spoke.

At last he gently raised the lid of the keyboard.

'Listen!' he said. 'I will play you no more of my own music – while I live – but this you may hear.'

Then slowly, solemnly, across the oppressive silence of the Minster rang out the dirge of Chopin's funeral March, played, surely, as it had never been played before.

'Herein is death,' said Cuthbert Ford, without looking at the cowering girl; and the dissolution of the body, the grave, the worm, were told in every note he touched.

'And herein is life eternal.'

The melody poured forth its appeal. Surely the organ spoke! Spirit voices called to spirit, telling of life that mocked the finality of earth. The world's passion, the world's pain, its petty hopes and fears, what were they to this? Come all ye that rejoice, come all ye that are weary, for here is your reward. O Death, where is thy sting; O Grave, where is thy victory?

It was as I followed thus the plaint of the organ, as the wonderful melody seemed to sink into my very being, destroying consciousness of all else, that I awoke – awoke to find myself in my own room, with Aylmer Vance bending over me a little anxiously.

For the last few minutes he had been trying to arouse me, but in vain. Never before had I been in so deep a sleep, never before had I had so intensely vivid a dream.

As soon as I was sufficiently recovered I told him all that I had seen and heard.

'What do you make of it?' I inquired eagerly, when I had finished – for there was no doubt in my mind that my vision had been a true representation of what had actually happened.

'It seems to me,' I went on, 'that this horrible creature, this perversion of a man, has made use of his wonderful gift of music to work upon some latent emotion in the girl's nature; he has palpably no influence over her except through the organ, and knowing this, it is by means of the organ he compels her to his will. If we can get him away, see that he is removed from Sandminster altogether, then the horrible, corrupting influence will be got rid of, and Miss Verriker should be restored to her normal senses. There is nothing she desires more ardently for herself, poor girl.'

But Aylmer's face remained very grave, and he did not seem disposed to fall in easily with the sanguine view which I had expressed.

Yet he was ready to agree that what I proposed was the only course that could be adopted.

Beryl came in to dinner that evening, and professed to be feeling ever so much better for her supposed rest.

She must have possessed a tremendous amount of self-restraint, for she gave no sign, in face or manner, of the strain which she had undergone.

But she left us early, and withdrew to her own room.

Over our cigars, later on, I related my vision to the colonel, who, although he did not say so in so many words, was rather disposed to regard it as a vision, and nothing more.

He was a man who had never in his life been brought face to face with anything outside the normal, and the idea of soul appealing to soul struck him, I have no doubt, as incongruous and impossible.

He accepted, however, our evidence as to the danger of Cuthbert Ford.

'I can see how it is,' he muttered. 'The fellow's got a wonderful gift of music, there's no doubt about that, and my girl has always been readily influenced by that sort of thing. I can remember, when she was a child, how she would stand and listen for hours together when her uncle, my brother, who was a fine pianist, would consent to play for her. And I've seen her, in later years, sobbing behind a hand-kerchief when I've taken her, at her request, to classical concerts, which, for my part, I found intensely boring. That's how the fellow's got hold of her, and I don't for a moment believe she can hear his music when it is inaudible to others. I expect she knows his habits, guesses when he will be playing. We may thank our lucky stars that he's such a parody of a man – had he been different, there might have been danger for her, real danger.'

Vance acquiesced, and I could see that he was glad the colonel should take this view – a view which seemed to be justified; or, in any case, it was evident that the organist was keeping his promise, for during the rest of our stay which was prolonged to quite a fortnight, nothing further occurred to mar the harmony of the household.

Cuthbert Ford was got rid of without any difficulty – indeed, he left Sandminster of his own accord, after Vance had secretly paid him a visit. But my friend returned from that visit with an expression upon his face that was by no means reassuring; he evidently anticipated some danger which I could only vaguely guess at.

And he begged Colonel Verriker to hurry on his daughter's marriage.

'The strength of a new affinity,' he said to me, 'that is the only hope. But is such an affinity possible? Dexter, I don't know – I don't know. And we – how utterly powerless we are!'

We returned to London, and though I did not forget my strange experience at Sandminster, I found my time fully occupied by other interesting experiences which cropped up as time went on.

Vance mentioned to me now and again that he had heard from Colonel Verriker, and that everything was going well, that Miss

Verriker was in the best of health, that her fiancé had returned to England, and that the marriage had been arranged to take place early in November.

And so the months passed, and eventually we received our invitation to the wedding. We were to go down and spend a week with the Verrikers, who proposed to have a full house for the occasion.

Vance appeared to be much relieved that the day of the ceremony was so close at hand. He repeated that he regarded this as the only safeguard for Beryl Verriker. She was in no danger, or so he maintained, as long as Cuthbert Ford lived and kept his promise; but Ford was a man with the seal of death upon his brow – and then – what then?

'A new and stronger affinity,' Vance repeated. 'I have no hope but that.'

And so, when the time came, we went to Sandminster, and found great preparations for the wedding going on, Colonel and Mrs Verriker happy and pleased with themselves, Beryl the picture of health and brightness, and Geoffrey Beynion, who was staying with some relations in the neighbourhood, and whom we now met for the first time, as fine a specimen of young English manhood as one could desire to see.

The wedding was to take place of the fifth day after our arrival, and on the third there was to be a big ball, at which all the best people in the county were to be present.

Of that ball, which duly took place, I need say nothing beyond this: that Beryl Verriker was easily the belle of it, and that she met with the admiration that she deserved.

The function was in every sense of the word a success, and there seemed to be not the smallest suggestion of cloud upon an horizon fair with promise for the future happiness of the young couple.

Upon the day following the ball, Miss Verriker, accompanied by Vance and myself, went for a spin in a new motor which her brother had just purchased, and which he drove himself.

We were on our way home, and were chatting and laughing together, while Vance, sitting in the front next to young Verriker, was turned towards us relating some amusing experience of the dance the night before, when, suddenly glancing at the girl's face, I realised that she was not listening to us, but that she was staring straight in front of her with a strained, unnatural look in her eyes.

I know that a cold shudder ran down my spine. I laid my hand upon hers with some idea in my mind of arousing her, and calling her back to herself, and the moment I touched her – strange as it may appear, I can swear to its truth – I seemed to hear, just as she must be hearing, the strain of a distant organ, the swelling of that weird, unnatural melody that I had once listened to in a dream.

The touch of my hand, however, had the effect of rousing her. I realised that she was struggling to conceal from us that there was anything wrong.

She spoke quite quietly, leaning forward and addressing her brother.

'Will you stop the car, Jim, and let me get out? I've just remembered that there are one or two shops I want to go to – a few things that I really must buy. No, I don't want you men to be with me, and we are quite close to home, so I can walk that little way back. You go straight on and have your tea – I'll have mine as soon as I get in.'

Verriker obeyed – he was always obedient to his sister's smallest request, and he did not suspect that there was anything amiss. Beryl descended from the car, and then, as we seemed to hesitate, said, with a suggestion of impatience:

'That's right, drive on, Jim, I shall be home quite soon.'

She had alighted at the corner of one of those narrow streets close to the Minster; our way home lay straight on. Vance and I exchanged troubled glances, but I left it to him to take the initiative – I did not dare to suggest any course of action myself.

Jim, I knew, had never been told of his sister's troubles.

Vance spoke not a word, and in another five minutes, or less, the car pulled up at the house, and we all descended; then, making some hurried excuse, Vance drew me aside.

His face was grave in the extreme, and his lips were set in a straight line.

'There's no time to be lost, Dexter,' he said. 'We must go to the church – we must follow her.'

It took us only a few minutes to reach the church, and we spoke not a word to each other upon the way. The great edifice appeared to be quite empty, and not a sound was to be heard. We turned our steps straight to the organ loft, and I had to strike a match as we mounted the narrow stairs, for the sun had already set, and it was quite dark in the narrow, confined space of the loft.

The organist, as we had expected, was there. He was seated upon the narrow bench, and his hands rested upon the keyboard, but his head and shoulders had fallen forward upon them, and he lay thus still, immobile, dead.

In the farther corner crouched Beryl Verriker, her hands clasped over her eyes, her whole body quivering and shaking.

It needed but an instant to take in the scene, then the match fell from my hand and we were plunged into darkness.

It was with difficulty that we got Miss Verriker home; she was half-fainting, and in an emotional, hysterical condition.

We placed her under the care of her mother, and, as soon as we were able, confided to the colonel everything that had happened.

And his answer was: 'Thank God the fellow's dead, so there's no further danger to be anticipated.'

I could see Vance smile grimly when he heard these words, but he uttered no protest, for what was the use of explaining to the good, simple-minded man that the real danger had only just come into being?

Upon inquiries being made we learnt that Cuthbert Ford had returned to Sandminster early that morning; he had been seen about the town, but no-one knew whence he had come, or what business had brought him back. But for us it was easy to conjecture that, knowing the imminence of death, he had elected to die beside his beloved organ.

His body was removed to the mortuary to await the necessary inquest.

The next day Beryl Verriker, as her father confidently predicted, seemed to be better. She had recovered her composure, but, watching her closely, I knew that she was not ignorant of her danger. And I remembered how Cuthbert Ford had threatened her – how he had declared that her immunity was only to last until his death – not after.

There was a suggestion of postponing the wedding for a few days, but she would have none of this, seeming to desire nothing so much as to give herself up to her future husband's care; only she stipulated that the full choral service which had been arranged for should be completely abandoned, and that the organ should on no account be played, not even for the traditional Wedding March.

'I couldn't stand it,' she shuddered; and, indeed, under the circumstances of the tragic death, her decision seemed only right and proper.

And so the fateful time arrived. The Minster was filled with a gaily-dressed crowd. The bridegroom paced nervously up and down in his allotted place.

People smiled at his anxious face, deeming it due to mere personal nervousness.

The hum of carefully-modulated voices filled the church. The news that the service was not to be choral had gone abroad, and the people who had come from a distance were asking the reason. I heard the explanation given by a well-informed gentleman sitting just in front of me, who whispered it to his friends.

'It's because that extraordinary creature, Cuthbert Ford, who used to be organist here, was found dead in the organ loft only yesterday. It was a bit of a tragedy – awkward thing to happen in the church, you know. The organ has not been touched since. I suppose they decided not to do so till the poor fellow is buried.'

Suddenly a murmur from pew to pew: 'The bride is coming!'

Beryl passed up the aisle leaning on her father's arm. 'Why, what is the matter with her?' Surprised comment followed her as she advanced. 'She is the very spectre of herself. Surely she isn't marrying a man she does not love?'

The guests farther removed from the aisle craned their necks to see.

Beryl, looking neither to right nor left, passed on, and stood impassive by the side of the bridegroom. So she remained through the service which followed, considerably cut as short as possible.

It was over, they were made man and wife, and the register was signed. A little colour stole into Beryl's pale cheeks as she emerged from the vestry, and she looked up and smiled at her husband.

She was smiling, too, as they came abreast of the altar and took up their position at the head of the procession.

'Why, she looks happy, after all!' murmured somebody close beside me. 'What a pity it is that there is no-one here to play the Wedding March!'

The first steps down the aisle were taken, and then, suddenly, the solemn silence of the great church was rudely broken.

Surely the strangest, most incongruous sound that ever greeted a wedding party!

Loud and resonant through the vaulted aisles of the church rolled forth the thunder of the first bars of Chopin's Funeral March. The first bars only, but they were sufficient to express the presence of death.

Scarcely a second, it seemed, the sound had been there clear in the ears of all; but even as every member of that assembly tried to grasp the meaning of it, straining ears to the utmost, they found themselves listening, not to sound, but to a speaking silence.

Women turned pale and sank back in their seats; men muttered beneath their breath. Could the senses of all have been deceived?

The bridegroom clutched his wife's arm and hurried on; anything to escape from the church.

She staggered rather than walked, and soon he was supporting almost her whole weight. So the broken procession approached the west door, in the gallery above which was placed the great organ.

Then, gently at first, but clear to the hearing of all, the swell of the organ rose again; but this time it was the melody of the Grand March, speaking of life and spiritual love, that was vaguely suggested to the hearer, and every note of it was a passionate appeal. How passionate, how intense, none knew, perhaps, but the bride, for she alone understood.

To all others it came as a shock, an insult, an abomination; to her it was a summons.

She stood rigid, her arms extended to the organ. Then, as the melody – no earthly melody, as it seemed now – rose to its full cadence, and died away in a quivering sigh, she fell to her knees.

'The call – the call!' she murmured; and as her husband raised her in his strong arms and bore her out, he heard her whisper gently: 'I come!'

It was rumoured afterwards that someone had gained access to the organ loft and played an evil practical joke. It is also possible for people to die from sudden fright.

Thus do we humans slur over what we cannot understand. For me, it was the sense of our utter impotence that appalled.

'Why had this evil thing to be?' I demanded of Vance.

There was some measure of comfort in his reply.

'We do not know that it was really an evil thing. Is it not possible that, in our ignorance, we appraise far too highly these poor bodies of ours? What do we know of our souls and of the laws that govern spiritual existence? May it not be that for some inscrutable reason it was necessary that those two souls should be brought together – that it was the appointed time for their union? And though the man's body was warped and hideous – though his mind may have been as ugly as his body – who shall judge of the soul panting for freedom? Not you or I, Dexter.' He placed his hand affectionately upon my arm. 'The laws of this world are not the laws of the hereafter. Some day the truth will be revealed.'

The Fear

One morning in late summer Aylmer Vance, after glancing through his correspondence, remarked that there was a gentleman coming to see us that day who would probably have something interesting to communicate.

'His name is Robert Balliston, and he's by way of being a millionaire,' explained Vance. 'A self-made man, so I understand. He's had a letter of introduction to me through some mutual friends, and he appears to be in great trouble about a house which he has recently taken on a long lease.'

'Have you any idea what form the trouble takes?' I inquired.

Vance shook his head. 'No,' he responded, 'I haven't been told anything about it yet. But I understand it's so serious that Mr Balliston and his family have had to turn out after being in residence barely a month. No doubt we shall hear all about it when he comes.'

In the course of the morning Mr Balliston put in his appearance. Somehow I think I could have guessed at once that he was a man who had made a lot of money by his own endeavours – he was so exactly the type one would expect. Coarse, but withal kindly-faced; thin hair – still dark – that scarcely hid his shining scalp; overdressed; rotund of figure as of pocket-book – we have all met his like many a time. His loud voice filled the room.

'Mr Vance,' he said, 'you are a man whose name is well-known to me, though, upon my word, I never expected to meet you in your professional capacity.'

Vance and I exchanged a glance, for there is nothing that my friend dislikes more than to be described as a 'professional'. He is a dilettante in every sense of the word, and has never in his life undertaken a research except for the sheer love of the thing. But it was impossible to be in the least offended with Mr Balliston.

'You are, sir, I believe, an authority on ghosts,' resumed the latter. He spoke the last word in a tone of depreciation almost comic.

Level-headed Robert Balliston and ghosts! – the conjunction of ideas seemed quite ridiculous.

'On what you call ghosts,' corrected Vance gently, 'perhaps I am.'

'I don't call 'em anything, sir,' snapped the millionaire. 'I don't believe in 'em, there aren't any such things. I've been told so all my life, and my father was a businessman like myself. Yet a funny thing has happened to me, and as it seems to be in your line I got my friends, the Whittakers, to give me an introduction. And I needn't say that I'm pleased to make your acquaintance as well as that of Mr Dexter.'

Of course we acknowledged the compliment, and then Aylmer Vance proceeded to inquire the source of the trouble.

'Well, it's this,' was the reply. 'How would you like it, Mr Vance, if you had leased a house – spent a great deal of money on it, too – and then had to leave it in a hurry, without any particular prospects of going back? Pleasant, isn't it? One may be well off, but there are limits.'

'Was it a new house?'

'New? No, old as they make 'em. Dates back to I don't know what period. Never was good at that sort of thing myself. Moated grange kind of place, you know. It was my wife's idea. She said when we had made enough we should take a big house and become county people. I heard of Camplin Castle from an agent, who said that it was just what we wanted – Lord of the Manor, good style of neighbour, and the rest of it. It's in Hampshire, near the borders of the Forest, not far from the sea. A fine, imposing place I found it, but out of repair. It hadn't been occupied for quite a time, as the price was so stiff. That put me on my mettle, I suppose, and I closed the bargain. Well, it took more repairing than I thought, and I spent quite a lot of money on it before we moved in. That's not a month ago, and here we are.' He spread out his hands with a despondent gesture.

Vance regarded our visitor critically.

'A man like you wouldn't give in easily,' he observed. 'Now what was it that drove you away, Mr Balliston?'

'That's just what beats me,' cried the other. 'I don't know. We've seen nothing, heard nothing – at least, not in the ordinary sense of the word. Every room is as comfortable as money can make it. But we couldn't stay in the castle, and the only explanation I can give is that we were frightened away.'

'And what frightened you?'

'Don't I say I haven't an idea? Every one of us in turn got seized with an unaccountable sense of fear. It's very difficult to explain, and all I know is that it's there, and that you can't fight against it. The feeling you get is of an invisible presence that is itself suffering from fear, a fear that is imparted to you. The thing, whatever it may be, radiates fear, if I may put it so.'

'And is this fear confined to one place, or to any particular time?'

'No, that's just the worst of it. If it were, we could avoid the place, for the castle's so big that I shouldn't in the least mind shutting up any particular room. But it happens at all manner of times and anywhere.'

'You say that you have all felt it. How many are you in family, Mr Balliston?'

'My wife and myself and our four children, two girls and two boys, ranging in age from twelve to eighteen. Our youngest child got it first – she's a girl of twelve, and we put her and her sister into two rooms communicating with each other. It was the very first night after we moved in. Gertrude – that's the eldest girl – heard her little sister sobbing, and when she went to find out what was the matter the child told her that she couldn't sleep, she was too frightened. She couldn't say what she was frightened of, and Gertrude laughed at her and told her not to be a little goose. But the child wouldn't stop crying, and so, to soothe her, Gertrude got into bed with her. And then she felt it too. She said it was awful. She snatched up little Myra and carried her to the other room, and there they both lay, shivering and trembling with the recollection of it, till the morning, when they told us what had happened.'

'And did anyone else ever sleep in that room?'

'Yes, we tried it one after another, at least, my two sons and I did, and we found it just as they had said. So we decided not to occupy that room any more, as there seemed to be something queer about it, and it would have been all right if things had not developed in another direction.'

'You got the same impression in other parts of the house?'

'Yes. A day or two later my wife had hysterics in the drawing-room; she said that she felt certain there was something going to happen to her, and it was a long time before she came round. Then one of the servants pitched down the stairs and hurt herself badly. It was rather late, and she was going up to bed. She said that there was something following her, and she knew it meant mischief. And so it went on, everybody was affected, and sometimes it caught several of us together. The sensation never lasted long, but it always made one feel as if one couldn't get through it alive. And so that's why we've left Camplin Castle, Mr Vance, and that's why I've come to consult you.'

Vance reflected for a few moments, then he inquired:

'Do you know anything of the history of Camplin Castle, Mr Balliston?'

'Very little. It didn't interest me, you understand. And we hadn't time to get to know any of the neighbours.'

'But you must of course, be acquainted with the name of the owner?'

'Yes. Camplin has belonged for hundreds of years to the Oswald family – the last of them died about a dozen years ago. He was never married, and there is no heir in the direct line. The present owner is a nephew and he is too poor to live in the place himself – at least, that's what the agent told me.'

'And didn't you try to get any more information from the agent?'

'Catch him giving me any!' was the somewhat scornful response. 'The man had done his deal and pocketed his commission. He wasn't likely to tell me anything against the place, and quite right, too, from a business point of view.'

Vance put a few more leading questions, and then informed Mr Balliston that he and I would go down to Camplin Castle the next day.

'I suppose there is someone on the premises to look after us?' he inquired.

'Yes, there's the lodge-keeper and his wife. I couldn't get any of the other servants to remain. I'll wire to Smith to expect you.' With a sudden burst of confidence Mr Balliston added: 'For heaven's sake, Mr Vance, find out the cause of the mystery. I tell you I was so frightened that the hair stood up on my head!'

I was trying to picture Mr Balliston's thin hair taking on this peculiar disposition as he took his leave.

The next day we travelled down to Camplin Castle, which we found to be situated several miles from the nearest station.

Mr Balliston had arranged for a motor car to be placed at our disposal for as long as we cared to stay. It was to be garaged at the village close by.

The sun was setting when we reached the gates of the park, which were opened for us by a somewhat surly and reticent lodge-keeper. He mounted the box by the side of our chauffeur, after informing us that his wife was at the castle making preparations for our reception.

Neither of them slept at the house, which we were to have quite to ourselves.

We passed down a fine avenue of elms, and presently, on either side, appeared great stretches of well-kept lawns and carefully-planted flower beds – every indication of the expenditure of much money.

A sweep of the road brought us to the house, which was a huge grey pile of varied architecture. Yet the whole effect was one of symmetry. In the centre appeared a timeworn, ivy-covered tower, round which the rest of the edifice had sprung up.

A neat, comfortable-looking woman admitted us to a vast hall, and thence to a dining-room, where the table was laid for dinner.

Vance spoke a few words of compliment on the arrangements that had been made for our comfort.

'You will look after us, I suppose, during our stay?' he remarked to Mrs Smith.

'Oh, yes, sir, as long as I don't have to remain at night,' was the response. 'I don't mind it so much otherwise.'

'It?' queried Vance, looking at her keenly.

'Yes, sir, the Fear. One never knows when it may come. I felt it this afternoon, but it passed quickly. At night, oh, it's terrible at night. I think Smith has taken your bags to your rooms,' she added hurriedly, as if to change the subject.

At this moment Smith reappeared, evidently anxious to take his departure. His more self-possessed wife conducted us upstairs to two large adjoining rooms on the first floor.

'It was Mr Balliston's instructions, gentlemen, that these rooms should be prepared for you tonight. This one that we are now in' – she seemed to be looking over her shoulder with an expression of tremulous nervousness – 'is the one in which nobody has been able to sleep. It's a long time now since it has been occupied at all.'

'Do you know anything of the story of this house, Mrs Smith?' inquired Vance.

'No, sir. We are London people. Mr Balliston brought us down.'

'But the village folk, don't they talk?'

'Well, sir,' was the answer, given in a faltering tone, 'of course we have heard all manner of stories, Smith and I, but there isn't one of them that really explains the Fear. You see, nobody had ever heard of it before Mr Balliston took the Castle. The house had stood empty ever since old Mr Luke Oswald died, and he only used to occupy a few rooms in the south wing. He was a queer old gentleman, they say, and lived quite by himself except for one servant, and he wouldn't ever see any company, so that people got to calling him a miser and whatnot. The old servant, whose name was Somers – John Somers – died soon after his master, but his grandson is living in the village – he is a builder by trade, and I should think he could tell you more than anyone else about the Oswald family, if you cared to go and have a chat with him.'

'I certainly shall make a point of doing so,' replied Vance, 'and thank you very much, Mrs Smith, for the information.'

With which he dismissed the good woman, who bustled away evidently pleased at being able to take her departure from the dreaded room.

I think I have said that our rooms had a communicating door between them – they were the ones originally occupied by Robert Balliston's two daughters.

The 'haunted room' – I will define it as such – was the smaller, and I imagine that the larger one – which I was to occupy – may have once been a boudoir. It was a bright, cheerful room, with windows looking out upon the front. Both apartments were quite modern in appearance, and had no suggestion of ghostly influence about them. They had evidently been quite recently furnished and decorated with good taste and the expenditure of plenty of money.

It struck me that the only antique piece of furniture was the bed in the smaller room, and this was of handsomely carved oak, surmounted by a high canopy.

I commenced unpacking my portmanteau, talking to Vance all the time through the open door. I could not see him, but could hear him moving about.

'We must certainly go to the village tomorrow and make some inquiries of this man Somers,' he was saying. 'I want to know – '

Suddenly he ceased speaking, and I thought I heard a sound like a stifled gasp, and then there came a deep silence.

I was seated by my dressing-table. I was about to turn and ask what was the matter when suddenly a cold breath seemed to pass across my face and I became riveted where I sat; I could not have looked round to save my life, though I felt that there was something there just behind me.

I could not utter a sound, my tongue seemed to cleave to a dry palate. I knew that I was trembling, filled with a sensation, a terrible pervading fear of impending death, a feeling that long fingers were about to grip me by the neck from behind and squeeze the life out of me. If not now, immediately, I knew that it must come soon, that a death, swift and cruel and terrible, awaited me.

I grasped the arms of the chair, and during that ghastly second a very eternity seemed to pass over me.

At last relief came. I felt the cold breath upon my face once more, and the next moment I was able to turn my head. Aylmer Vance stood in the doorway between our rooms.

I put my hand to my forehead and found the hair wringing wet.

'So you've had a turn, too?' asked Vance with a quiet smile. 'It isn't pleasant, is it?'

I vowed that it was anything but pleasant. I think I swore lustily.

'What does it mean?' I inquired.

'That's what we've got to find out,' he replied, looking at me with some anxiety. 'Whatever it is it seems to have passed from my room to yours – as if it follows the course of some invisible being – a being that is afraid, horribly afraid, and that is able to impart its fear to anyone who comes in its way. It's a ghastly kind of experience, Dexter, and it will no doubt be worse at night. Are you prepared to go through with it?'

I grasped his hand and said I was. But I must admit that I was anything but happy in my mind.

Mrs Smith looked at us curiously when we appeared for dinner, but made no remark. The meal over, she took her departure, promising to be round early in the morning to give us our breakfast.

After dinner we sat and smoked for a while, and then, as the night was oppressively hot, we made our way to the garden.

It was really delightful to escape for a short time from the evil influence which seemed to pervade the house – even in the absence of the actual overwhelming terror. One felt – one knew – that something horribly, abominably cruel must have been enacted within the walls of the Castle, and that, however long ago it may have been, the impression had never been eradicated.

The night air was deliciously cool and balmy with scented air. It was rather dark, though the sky was rich with stars. Our walk was not objectless. Vance wanted to explore the house on the outside and at night.

Twice we made the circle of it. There were broad terraces to most of the wings, but at the back, beneath the tower, there was only a narrow strip of lawn flanked by a shrubbery.

There were a few windows in the tower, but quite high up there seemed to be a circular apartment with several windows, and one of these stood wide open. And while we were looking up at it the Fear overtook us once more, although, on this occasion, it was only of a very transitory nature and disappeared altogether as soon as we were able to leave the spot.

When, a few minutes later, we mustered up courage to return, there was no recurrence of the ghastly feeling, but as we stood there, waiting for it, Vance suddenly placed his hand upon my shoulder, and pointing up to the tower exclaimed:

'Look there, Dexter. Do you notice anything strange?'

I looked and realised at once that the window, which had stood open only a few minutes ago, was now closed – yet, as we knew, the house was absolutely untenanted.

'What is the time, Dexter?' asked Vance in a tone that, for him, was almost excited. 'I think it is of importance.'

I struck a match and looked at my watch. It was then half-past eleven.

We returned to the house after this experience, and I knew that I was glad of a stiff peg of whisky and soda – for it wasn't as if the terrors of the night were at an end.

There was still the haunted room to be faced.

But Vance would not allow me to share this room with him as I offered to do. My nerves were already sufficiently on edge, he declared, and though I protested, I must admit that I allowed myself to be easily persuaded. I insisted, however, that the communicating door between the two rooms should be left open so that I might be summoned, if necessary, at any moment.

And so we retired for the night, though, as far as I was concerned, it was not to sleep. I lay tossing about in my bed, expecting at every moment to hear Vance's call, and at last, unable to bear the strain any longer, I got up and went into his room to see how he was faring.

To my surprise, I found him sleeping calmly and peacefully. He had a shaded light burning beside the bed, and he did not stir when I approached. It was evident that the Fear had not assailed him, for I was quite sure he could not have slept through it if it had.

I tiptoed back to my room, and lay down again, and soon afterwards, my mind relieved, I got off to sleep, and did not open my eyes until I was aroused by the sun shining in at the window.

Vance was already up and dressing, and when he heard me astir he called out to know how I had slept.

'I've had a remarkably good night myself,' he said cheerfully. 'Not a sign of the Fear or of anything else.'

'And yet other people have been unable to sleep in that room!' I exclaimed wonderingly. 'How do you account for that, Vance?'

He shrugged his shoulders.

'I can't account for it – yet,' he replied. 'We must wait and see what happens tonight. I've got a theory, but I'll keep it to myself at present.'

'Well, I claim my turn to sleep there tonight,' I declared, for in the sunlight my courage was completely restored. 'Perhaps my faculty of seeing visions may be of service in solving the mystery.'

We found that Mrs Smith had provided us with an excellent breakfast, and though I am sure she wanted to question us, she did not venture to do so directly, nor did Vance or I show ourselves responsive to her hints.

We spent the morning exploring the Castle, and, as may be expected, it was to the tower that we first turned our attention.

We mounted to the circular room near the summit by means of a winding staircase to which access was obtained from the portrait gallery.

The room had been furnished, evidently by Mr Balliston, in semi-oriental fashion, and the walls, of great age, were hung with tapestry. Somehow the impression of modernity jarred. We soon localised the window which we had seen open the night before. It was now closely shut. It was large and heavy, and we found that it was only with difficulty and by our united efforts, that we could raise the sash. Looking out, we saw beneath the little shrubbery where we had received the impression of fear.

There was nothing, however, by which the mystery might be elucidated, and we could only decide to make a further investigation when night came on.

In the afternoon we made our way to the village and inquired for Mr Somers, the builder.

Unfortunately, he was absent for the day, so all we could do was to leave a message making an appointment for the next morning. We made certain other inquiries, but learnt little more than we already knew.

With the exception of Mr Somers, no-one in the village – at least no-one that we could find – had been inside the Castle while it stood empty. Stories had, of course, got abroad, but they were indefinite, and did not touch upon the Fear. Mr Somers's father and grandfather had both been reticent men, while the builder himself was apparently loath to admit that there was anything wrong. In fact, he made light of what had become common talk.

We returned to the Castle towards six o'clock, and were again caught by the Fear in our rooms at the same time as the night before. All that we could determine was that it certainly passed from the smaller to the larger room and then went out to the passage. We felt it quite distinctly just outside the door.

After that we proceeded to the tower room and made sure that all the windows were firmly closed.

We dined, attended by Mrs Smith, as on the night before, but we retired early to our bedrooms, for Vance wished to put his theory to the test. He explained his undisturbed sleep of last night by the possibility that the Fear, which everyone had experienced who slept in that room, came on earlier – before he went to bed – and that consequently he had missed it.

'Mr Balliston did not say that anyone spent the whole night in that room,' he remarked.

It was decided that I should occupy the 'haunted room'. I lay down accordingly, practically fully dressed, on the outside of the bed, and Vance sat up in the other room, with the light full on, reading a book. It was then about half-past ten.

And half an hour later the Fear assailed me.

I have already described the sensation, so I need not repeat it, except to say that tonight it seemed increased a hundredfold.

I lay perfectly rigid, fully conscious of Vance's propinquity in the next room, but voiceless, absolutely unable to call out to him for assistance. My forehead was wringing wet with perspiration, and all my being was strung up with expectation – the expectation of something imminent, something ghastly, something inevitable.

And then, of a sudden, though there was nothing to be seen, absolutely nothing, I received the impression that the bed upon which I lay was already occupied – that someone else was lying there, someone who trembled and shook and sobbed so that the whole structure seemed to quiver beneath me.

I reached out my hand, but it encountered nothing, and yet I knew – I knew.

I cannot say how long I lay thus. It seemed to me an eternity – it may in reality have been a quarter of an hour. And the most awful part of it was the sense of helplessness, and the fact that instead of passing off as it had done on the other occasions, the Fear seemed to be increasing, to be growing momentarily more intense. Every successive moment was charged with acuter agony. Something was going to happen, and it was going to be now – now, at once.

I found myself sitting up upon the bed, straining my ears to listen for the approach of the danger. Perhaps my power of visualising things added to the intensity of the emotion, for I knew that I myself underwent every tiny detail of the agony that was endured by some-one who had occupied that bed in years long gone by, and whose presence I vaguely felt by my side.

And as I sat thus it seemed to me that certain sounds fell upon my ears, and yet I cannot assert that they existed except through some impression mysteriously imparted to my brain.

Had there been any reality about them they were certainly loud enough to have disturbed Vance, who sat in his room quietly reading on, totally unconscious of the torture that I was enduring.

I thought I heard the furtive opening and closing of a door below and then a stealthy step upon the stair drawing nearer and nearer, and it seemed to me, as I listened, that I gave vent to a wild scream of terror – and yet I know now that not a sound escaped my lips.

Like all other impressions of those ghastly moments, the scream was a suggested product of my own brain – just as was the feeble crying of a child that I heard at the same moment, the frightened wail of an infant disturbed in its sleep.

And now I could hear laboured breathing in the passage outside, and the next moment it was at the door.

I felt a strange tingling at the roots of my hair, and the sudden recollection flashed through my brain of what Mr Balliston had said: 'I assure you it made my hair stand on end!'

A suggestion that had amused me at the moment, but now I understood it – if Mr Balliston had gone through one tithe of what I was enduring.

I gazed with horror-riveted eyes at the door, and presently it seemed that the handle moved as if it were being slowly turned; then I was vaguely conscious of another shriek, louder by far than the first, and this was followed, to my acutely sharpened perception, by a sound as if someone had sprung from the bed by my side and was pattering across the floor with bare feet in the direction of the room occupied by Vance.

And all the while I could hear the whimpering of the child, carried, as it seemed, by the owner of the running feet, into the adjoining room.

The next moment the spell was broken – the terror had passed from me, and I lay there, panting and gasping, struggling to recover my shattered senses.

I had regained the use of my limbs, and blindly, wildly, following some impulse which I could not for the moment account for, I sprang from the bed and rushed into my friend's room.

Vance was sitting immobile in his chair, and the book which he had been reading had dropped to the floor. His face was drawn and troubled, and his eyes were intently fixed upon the door leading into the passage.

And I knew that the Fear was upon him, that it had passed from my room to his.

'It's there at the door,' he whispered. 'Do you feel it too, Dexter? It's there at the door.'

I felt it afresh. I knew that someone was struggling to open the door from the inside, to turn a key which appeared to resist the nerveless, frightened fingers.

And there was the whimpering of the child too.

And then it passed away. Vance sprang to his feet, and we stood gazing at each other for one distracted moment.

Then, like myself, a few moments before, he seemed to pull himself together.

'Dexter,' he muttered hoarsely, 'we must follow.'

Without pausing for my reply he made for the door, tore it open, and together we rushed out into the darkness of the passage.

Luckily he had his electric lamp with him, otherwise we should never have found our way along those little-known corridors and staircases, enveloped as they were in complete obscurity.

And it must be remembered that we were not following anything that we could actually see or hear – we were following the thread of terror that by some inconceivable means was imparted to our brains.

On we went, and we knew that we were following something that was following something else – a wild, cruel chase in which the pursued, in a very agony of terror, sought vainly for some means of escape.

And so, across the picture gallery, we came to the tower, and eventually to the room at its summit.

A breath of night air blew in upon my forehead. The window stood wide open, and it was there that the Fear reached its climax, though to the normal sense perfect stillness reigned – the whole room seemed to me full of horrid sound.

Vance and I were rooted to the spot where we stood while some abominable tragedy, only dimly guessed at, was played out to its culmination.

And then the window slid softly down, and all was over.

And it was well that it was so, for it seemed to me that another moment of such strain would have sent me mad. I looked at Vance and noticed the great beads of perspiration upon his forehead, the ghastly pallor of his face, the quivering of his hands and his shoulders – he had felt the terror no less than I.

'It's all over,' he muttered; 'it's gone!'

'Thanks God for that!' I panted in reply. 'Let's get away, Vance, for fear that it may recur. I – I couldn't stand it any more.'

'It won't recur tonight,' he replied, trying to force a smile. 'But let's go down to the dining-room, Dexter, and have some brandy and a smoke. That will steady our nerves.'

I was very glad to act upon this suggestion, and a stiff dose of brandy soon put me to rights again.

And then I told Vance of all I had gone through in the earlier part of the night; how I had lain there upon the bed, unable to call out to him, while the Fear gradually possessed me.

'What do you make of it?' I inquired.

He shrugged his shoulders and remarked that at present we could do little but conjecture.

'It's to be hoped that tomorrow may bring light,' he continued; 'that is, if we can persuade Mr Somers to speak.'

We spent an hour, however, discussing our own theories, which, as it turned out, were not very far from the truth, and eventually we went back to bed, where our sleep was undisturbed for the rest of the night.

The next day we sought out Mr Somers, whom we found to be a young man of rather taciturn disposition; nevertheless, he eventually yielded to the charm of Aylmer Vance's manner, and consented to tell us all he knew, after exacting a promise that, for his own family reputation, the story should not be published abroad.

'But, indeed, gentlemen,' he said, 'if you can do anything to stop the horror – to clear Camplin Castle of its ghosts – I shall be grateful to you, and glad I have spoken. You see, my grandfather – but I'd better tell you the story.'

And so, sitting there in the little shop parlour to which he had led us, we listened to the story of Camplin Castle, or, rather, to the portion of it that was of interest to us at that moment.

Camplin Castle had belonged to the Oswald family for centuries. For years and years it was handed down from father to son, and nothing had occurred to break the succession till about the middle of the nineteenth century, when the then owner of the estate, Jasper Oswald, quarrelled with his eldest son, Luke, who was a wild young fellow and had contrived to offend his father deeply. Luke ran away from home before he was twenty-one, and at last a report was received that he was dead.

So, on the death of Jasper, the younger brother, Philip succeeded to the estate.

Philip had a beautiful wife, whose name was Elen, and a child, of whom they were both inordinately fond – a little boy of two. He was a passionate, ambitious man, was Philip, imbued with the violent temper that was characteristic of the Oswalds.

But Luke, the elder son, was not really dead, and soon after Philip and his family were installed at the castle he returned to claim his own from his brother. They would not recognise him, said that he was an impostor, and when he took his case to the Law Courts he lost it. He could not wholly prove his identity at the time, and it was suggested that Philip was able to suborn evidence against him.

Well, Luke came up to the house and saw his brother after the case was over. Philip sat in the dining-room with his wife and child, and made the servants throw Luke out.

Then Luke turned and cursed him, swore that he would kill them all, and that he would not do it at once, but, as they had made him suffer, so should they suffer, too. The torture of Fear, fear of impending death, the knowledge that it might fall upon them at any moment, was to be their fate.

And they read in his face that he meant what he said.

From that day they knew no rest; the fear of death was constantly upon them. And so it was that fear, a fear which was drawn out for the best part of twelve months or more, that impregnated the walls of Camplin Castle, had reigned there ever since.

'And did Luke Oswald kill his brother?' inquired Vance.

The builder shrugged his shoulders.

'Philip Oswald died mysteriously about six months after the termination of the law case. He was found drowned in a pond, and it was assumed that he was killed by poachers, with whom he was constantly coming into conflict. But the murderer was never found.'

'And the wife and child?'

'Luke did not spare them, either. You see, it was not only revenge that he wanted. He wished to recover the estate for himself and his possible heirs. But nobody knows exactly what happened. Another six months went by, and then it was reported that Elen Oswald had gone mad, and that, in a fit of frenzy, she had thrown her child from a window in the tower, killing it at once. She was carried off to an asylum, where she died soon after. And then, some years later, Luke Oswald was able to bring evidence to show that he was indeed the rightful heir to Camplin Castle, and so he took possession and moved in, and it seemed at first as if he was going to live in luxury and in great style.

'But everything went wrong with him. He got engaged to a beautiful girl, but she died a few days before the wedding. And so he never married, and there was no child to succeed him, no Oswald to be lord of the manor after his death. And then, no-one could say why, but people shunned him; there was something in his appearance that set them against him – he was hard and cruel to his tenants, who loathed him, and would not work for him, so that his land went to waste. And by degrees health forsook him, too, and he would go about, worn and old before his time, with the appearance of a haunted man.

'No servants would stay with him at the castle – none, at least, except my old grandfather, who had been there in Philip's time, too, and who was a queer type of man, sullen and morose, and who was not afraid of God or devil. They shut up the best part of the castle, and lived in a few rooms only, seeing no-one and wanting to see no-one – a pair of recluses.

'And so, twelve years ago, Luke Oswald died, and the mystery of his life remained a mystery to the world outside. Camplin Castle passed into the hands of the next-of-kin, who was a distant cousin, a man who had no interests in the estate, and who bore another name. He came to Hampshire to view his new property, stayed there a few days, and then placed it in the hands of the house agents, took his departure, and has not been seen again in the neighbourhood.'

'You think that he had his experience of the Fear,' suggested Vance, 'and made the best of a bad bargain by attempting to let his property?'

'He gave out that he was too poor a man to live at the castle,' was the guarded reply, 'and I know nothing of what happened while he was actually in possession. My grandfather remained as caretaker until his death the following year, and it was upon his deathbed that he told my father things that my father only told me when he, in turn, was dying, begging me to keep the secret for our honour's sake.'

'And you can tell us this secret?' asked Vance gently.

The young man flushed.

'Let it be a hint,' he said. 'My grandfather, while in Mr Philip's service – and after his death, too – was in the pay of Mr Luke. He connived at that year of terror. It was with his help that Luke obtained access to the castle whenever he wished. And' – he lowered his eyes – 'I do not think that the unfortunate woman threw her child from the window. Oh! do you wonder,' he added, with some display of emotion, 'that Camplin Castle is not habitable today, that it reeks with horror from cellar to attic?

'My advice to Mr Balliston,' he concluded, 'would be to raze the whole place to the ground, and to build a new house upon the site. Short of that, I don't see what he can do.'

'I'm inclined to think that our friend the builder's advice is good,' remarked Vance to me, after this interesting interview. 'So long as bricks and mortar, and the atmosphere itself, are retentive, as we know them to be, there is little, Dexter, that you or I, or anyone else, can do to be of assistance.

'And that's the worst of this hobby of ours,' he added, with a suggestion of sadness in his voice; 'for people come to us, as Mr Belliston did, begging for our assistance, and thinking that by some strange mysterious power we can lay the ghosts, or what they are pleased to call the ghosts. But that's just what we can't do; we can only prove what has been proved hundreds of times before, that there are more things in heaven and earth than the human philosophy of the present day can understand.

'And again and again I find the same advice recurring – the advice which Somers has given us – the advice of one who has not had the experience of years such as I have had, but which is quite as good as any that I can give – destroy. And that, too, is the advice that applies to Camplin Castle.'